The Father of My Children

by

Charles Okee Iwuala

Table of Contents

About the Author

Charles Okee Iwuala hails from
Umuduruokoro kindred of Umudiagba,
Abajah in Nwangele Local Government
Area of Imo State, Nigeria.

He obtained his B.A. degree in History &
International Relations from Imo State
University, but has a burning passion for
creative writing.

This novel is his second published work.
The first was his very successful novel: No
Man Is an Angel

Book Review

The Father of My Children is a story of how the idealistic expectations of a couple at the initial stages of their marriage relationship can be affected by fluctuations in their material fortune, depending on how they respond to the situations.

The story tells specifically how Syl, a 'Honey' and Darling Husband', is reduced to a contemptible Sylvanus a mere father of my children'

What happens in the end raises an inevitable question: "Who was to blame; the man or the woman?" The answer to the question lies within the reader's judgement.

The author gives the novel a compelling appeal as he situates the varied interesting episodes and phases of the story within familiar contemporary cultural contexts. His profuse use of Igbo proverbs and aphorisms to spice up his narrative, is characteristic of his unique style.

Chapter One

It was in the early part of June when farmlands were all lush with luxuriant growth of planted crops. The two o'clock sun was so harsh and scorching that one could hardly imagine that it would rain later in the day. They had finished working for the day, and she left the farm earlier to go and prepare lunch before her parents would return. Her parents had stayed back in the bush to fetch feed for their livestock (goats).

Walking on the dusty motorable road that formed a connect between the two major tarred roads in the area, with a bundle of firewood on her artistically plaited hair, a Toyota Land Cruiser jeep sped past her, but soon cleared to the roadside and pulled up. She nearly took to her heels, thinking it was a kidnapper, as kidnapping was the order of the day; but the smiles on the face of the young man who alighted from the cozy car had her completely dazed and captivated.

'Good afternoon, sir-!' she greeted as she
got to the place where the man had parked.

'Good afternoon!' replied the young man.
'Please,
young lady, can I've a minute of your time?'
'No, sir!' she retorted as she further
muttered, 'can't you see I'm carrying
something on the head?'

'Just a minute; and you will continue to
where you're heading to,' the young man
pleaded.

'Sir, I'm just coming from the farm; and
besides, I'm carrying something on the
head,' she stopped, turned and complained
bluntly with some strain on her face.

'I understand, but just one minute,' the
young man insisted.

In the end, she gave in; although she
refused to put down the load on her head,

even when the young man offered to help her do so. She knew that doing so would definitely prolong their discussion and she didn't have such time. Apart from the fact that she was going home to cook, she was afraid that her parents might meet her

there; and if they did, she would be in trouble. 'I'm Syl. What about you?' the man asked after introducing himself.

'My name is Serah,' replied the young girl. Wow! Seraphina! That's my sister's name,' he teased her.
Sincerely speaking, he didn't have any sister, let alone one that answered such a name. He said that just to make the young girl feel relaxed and less tense. At least, she could now talk to him without nervous fright.
'Do you have a sister that answers that name?' Serah asked enthusiastically.
'Yes, of course!' Syl replied and then added: 'She's schooling at Uniport.'

'Really!' Serah said, google-eyed.

'Yes, of course!' Syl said rather proudly.
'She's in third year and will be rounding off
in two years' time. She's studying Agric
Economics and, as you probably know, it's a
five-year course. What about you, Serah?
Where do you school? Unical?'

Serah went pop with laughter. 'If I tell this
man that since I was born I haven't been to
Calabar, not to talk of schooling in Unical,
he may not believe me,' she said in her
mind. However, she found it pretty difficult to
answer that question. She thought that
telling Syl she wasn't a student, indeed a
university student, might scare him away if
his motive was marriage.

Nonetheless, she would tell him the whole
truth, because, if she didn't and it turned out
that he was coming for marriage, he would
still find out the truth eventually. Then, it
would be counter-productive as Syl might

begin to see her as a liar; and one cannot
be in a serious relationship with someone
who doesn't tell the truth.

However, she had to be very tactful in
saying the truth so that it would not look as if
she didn't have interest in education,
whereas it was the financial handicap of her
family background that had debarred her
from going to a higher institution.

'I'm still awaiting my JAMB result', she thus
said. 'Ok, you're still a JAMBite,' Syl said,
while she nodded and that ended the topic.

'From which village are you, Serah?' Syl
further asked her.

She told him the name of her village. It was
the same place they met and her house was
just some metres away.

'What's the name of your family?' Syl asked
her. 'Iwuanyanwu,' she replied.

The name sounded novel to Syl. It was
neither one of the popular nor the notorious
families in the town.

'Could I have your phone number, Serah?'
Syl

requested.

'I don't have a phone,' Serah lied. That was
a white

lie, of course. The fact was that she didn't
like giving her phone number out, especially
to people she didn't know fully well.

Syl didn't insist on the phone number. He
had known the name of her family and could
trace her out with that. He offered to take
her home in his car, but Serah, in her usual
coy nature, coupled with the fear of her
parents, turned down the offer.

"Thank you,' she said.

'Let me take you home,' Syl insisted. 'No, don't bother,' she said as she ended the dialogue abruptly with: 'Ok, bye!'

Instantly she turned her back on Syl and walked away from the scene. Syl stared at her with utter incredulity as she walked out on him. He didn't talk further, but merely nodded, as if telling himself: "Honestly, this is the kind of girl I need, a gin that is not easily moved by material things." When she had gone a little far, though still
within sight, Syl entered his car and drove off.

All these happened on a Friday.

On the following day, as the dew drizzled in the early hours of the morning, Innocent, his wife and their three children left altogether for the farm. They had been repeating the same practice for the past one week, and their motive was to complete their weeding work before the rainy season (which was already around the corner) would set in, in full force.

Later, Serah was asked by her mother to go back home to give some money to one of their neighbours who was going to a distant market so that the woman would help them buy some foodstuff. As she was in the house combing her mother's handbag for the money, a car drove into her father's compound, hooting its horn. She peeped out through the edge of the window and discovered it was a red jeep: the same car she met on her way back from the farm on the previous day.
She would not want to come out to receive the visitor, considering the lowly nature o her father's house: a two-room mud house with thatched roof which was leaking all over But come to think of it, the fellow that came might be one of the people who didn't like marrying from blue-blood families,

perhaps a "deux ex machina" whom God
had sent to salvage the financial status of
her lowly birth.

After due consideration, Serah abandoned
what she was doing in the house and came
out.
'Hi, Serah!' Syl hailed her when she finally
emerged.
'Good morning, sir!' she greeted, though
very coldly.

'Good morning; and how are you?'
'I'm fine."
'And your parents?'
"They're fine too.' 'Hope they're at home?'
'No-o! They have gone to the farm.'
'So early?'
'Sure! In fact, you wouldn't have met me at
home but for the fact that my mum sent me
back home on an errand.'
'Really?'

'Yes, of course, we usually leave home very early so that by the time the scorching sun is up, we're done with much of the day's work.'

'It's ok,' Syl submitted and further asked: 'When do you think I can come back and meet your dad and mum at home?'

'Mmm, let's say by evening,' Serah said, 'but, sir, if I may ask, what are you coming to meet them for?'

Syl smiled and said, 'Don't worry, Serah, when I come back in the evening, you'll get to know what my Mission is'. 'Okay-o!' Serah said. 'But, Sir, you had better tell me, so that I know exactly what you're coming for.'

'Just don't worry. When I come back...you'll know...,' Syl repeated. 'Okay!' she said as she shrugged her shoulders. 'Alright, till then,' he said. 'Okay then,' she responded.

'Bye!' he finally said before he turned and walked towards his car.

When they came back from the farm, Innocent took his bath; and after his lunch of yam and pepper soup, he took his easy chair to under a pepper fruit tree, right in front of his house. As he sprawled himself on the chair, he soon saw a red jeep advance slowly towards his house.

'Who's this?' he muttered as he sat up staring at the cozy car with utter surprise. In fact, throughout the period he had lived in that place, he had never seen such a big car come into his compound, except one day, a man in a Mercedes Benz car missed his way and mistakenly drove into the compound.

Syl pulled up a few meters away from the pepper fruit tree and turned off the ignition. Alighting from the car, he went up to where

Papa Serah was sitting. As he advanced gently toward the old man, Papa Serah stared at him just the same way he had stared at the car.

'Nna-anyi-ukwu!' Syl called him, now standing before him, with a smiling face. 'Nnaa!' Papa Serah responded, meanwhile stretching out his right arm for a hand-shake with Syl, while still staring at his face. 'Good afternoon, sir!' Syl greeted, shaking hands with him.
'Afternoon!' Papa Serah replied and then added: "Nnaa, please pardon me, I can't quite identify you.'

Syl smiled and introduced himself, saying, 'Nna-anyi

ukwu, I'm from Amata.' 'Where in Amata?' Papa Serah asked him very enthusiastically.

'I'm from Ohaka family,' Syl replied 'Who's your father in the family?' 'Livinus, sir!' 'Livinus Ohaka?' "Yes, Sir!'

Papa Serah stretched out his hand for another hand shake with him. Meanwhile, he called one of his younger daughters and asked her to bring him a seat for the visitor. 'Your father was my schoolmate,' Papa Serah told Syl. 'Really?' Syl screamed excitedly and goggle-eyed. 'Yes of course!' Papa Serah proudly affirmed. All of us schooled together at Saint Theresa Grammar School. Then, your father was among the smaller boys in our class.'

As the introduction was still on, Chidinma re emerged with a plastic chair and kept it near her father.

'Nnaa, sit down!' Papa Serah said, pushing the chair over to Syl. 'Thank you, sir,' Syl said as he got himself seated on the chair.

At this juncture, Papa Serah excused himself briefly to go into the house. Soon, he came back carrying a saucer and a small wooden stool. He kept the saucer on the stool which he had stood before the two of them.

In the saucer were two kola-nuts and a penknife. Papa Serah removed the knife and kept it on the stool. Then, he lifted the saucer up.

'Nnaa, here comes kola,' he said presenting the kola-nuts to Syl. The latter touched the saucer and said, 'Nna-anyi-ukwu, I've seen the kola; please bles it.'

Papa Serah said a brief prayer over the kola nuts took one of them and broke it with the pen knife. It had only two lobes. It was the Hausa kola nut species called gworo. He took one lobe and extended the saucer to Syl, who took the remaining lobe.

'Thank you, sir,' Syl said as he picked the lobe of kola-nut.

'You're welcome,' Papa Serah responded. He then urged Syl to take the second kola-nut away with him as Igbo custom holds that when a kola nut arrives home, it tells the story of where it is coming from.

As they ate the kola, Syl drew his seat closer to Papa Serah.

"Thank you, sir,' he said to him again. 'Thank you,' Papa Serah replied. Meanwhile, he was filled with suspense as he never knew yet what the visitor had up his sleeves.

'There's an Igbo adage which says that a frog does not run in broad day-light without a cause, Syl said, crossing his arms on his knees, with his head bent low. Papa Serah nodded in silent concurrence. 'It was yesterday as I was coming back from my friend's house,' Syl continued, 'that I got to that place,' he said pointing toward the place he met Serah, and saw a dark, young girl who was carrying firewood on her head. I drove past her, cleared to the road-side, turned off the ignition and waited till she came closer. I stopped her and asked her, her name. She told me. I then asked her where she hails from and she said she's from this village. I further asked her about her family and she told me.

'Today, I decided to come and see her parents and also tell them my mind concerning her. As a matter of fact, I came here in the morning. It was her that I met; and she told me that you and her mum had gone to the farm.' 'Yes, we left for the farm very early,' Papa Serah affirmed.

'That was what she told me also,' Syl said. 'But did she tell you I came?' he further asked. 'No, she didn't,' Papa Serah replied, shaking his head.

Perhaps, she forgot to tell you.'
'Maybe'

'So, Nna-anyi-ukwu, that's the reason why
I'm here,' Syl concluded, sitting up.

'You did well, my son,' Papa Serah
commended him, 'but if I may ask, before
you set out for this mission, did you confer
with your father?'

'Actually, I didn't,' Syl confessed shaking his
head. 'I said, let me come first to see
whether it's something that is going to work
out before bringing them along.'

'You also did well,' Papa Serah praised him
once more, but in all, you will have to go
back home. If you get home, tell your father
about your mission, that the girl in question
is the daughter of his old school mate,
Innocent Osuagbara of Umuike village.
Whatever he says, then, you know whether

or not to continue, because, according to
the Igbo, a fowl with deformed leg is never
sold nearer home.' 'Okay, sir,' I've heard
what you said.' Syl responded.
'Yes, if you get home, tell your father.
Whatever he says, then, we know what
next.'
'It's alright, sir. Let me be on my way home,'
he said as he stood up to go. 'Okay, my
son, greet your father,' Papa Serah said,
also standing up.

'Alright, sir!' said Syl as he turned to go to
his car. Just then, he recalled he had not
seen both Serah and her mother since he
came; but when he asked of them, Papa
Serah told him they went out, though Serah
was in the house. Since the mission was not
certain to be fruitful, there was no point
trying to sustain and strengthen the
acquaintance. In any case, Serah herself
was not ready to come out even if the
mission was going to be successful. It was
because her parents were not around when

Syl came in the morning that she decided to come out to meet him. Otherwise, she would have disappeared through the backyard and left him with her parents.

One day, a man on a Honda motorcycle saw her, just the way Syl did, and also traced her home to seek her hand in marriage. After the man was offered kola, he requested for her presence so that he could make his intention known to her parents; but when Serah was sent for, she ran away through the backyard. The man dusted up his buttocks and went back home in anger claiming he was not the kind of person that could be treated with such contempt. Serah, however, later cried her eyes out, saying she did not mean to turn the man down.

'I did what I did just to know whether he was a truly serious suitor,' she further explained.

Women often feel reluctant to accept even what they, inside them, are dying for. It is in their nature. Her mother, however, was the person tha actually went out to collect the fish she gave thei neighbour some money to buy for her.

'When they come back, greet them for me,' Sy said before he finally entered his car and drove off.

'Ok,' Papa Serah replied.

As he drove back home, he thought very much about his meeting with Papa Serah that afternoon more especially the adage the old man had used in the course of their discussion namely, A fowl with c deformed leg is never sold nearer home. He couldn't fathom the meaning of that expression, though he knew it was pregnant with meaning. Anyway, he would first tell his father, as Papa Serah had suggested.

Depending on what his father said, he would then, know what next to do.

When he got home, his father was in the veranda listening to four o'clock news with a four-battery radio set. The radio set, to which the old man had a sentimental attachment, had a rope which enabled him to hang it over his shoulder wherever he was going. Syl had once bought him a brand new radio set so that he could discard the old and out-dated one; but he refused to do so. According to him, that radio was his only property that followed him home from the civil war. 'In the effort to secure it; the Nigerian soldiers had nearly killed me,' he once said.

'Good afternoon, father,' Syl greeted him as he took his seat next to him. He didn't, however, tell him anything until he was done with the news.

The news was about how two policemen had fought over fifty naira "roger" offered to them by a bus driver and how they inflicted serious wounds on each other. At times, the wave would disturb the transmission of the news. Then, Papa Syl would carry the radio set up struggling to get the details of the news.

When he was done with the news, Syl then began to tell him about his journey to Umuike. He was very much excited to hear Syl say he had found a girl he would marry.

On several occasions, Syl's parents had brought him young girls to marry, but he would always reject them. At times, he would claim the girls were short. At other times, he would say they were too dark or too fair in complexion. Sometime, his mother had brought one girl from her maiden town, but he also turned that one down claiming she was too educated, as she possessed a university degree.

In truth, his sole reason for rejecting those girls brought by his parents was that none of them came from a lowly, humble background.

Some people believe that girls from blue-blood families would always nag when eventually they get married. This rather illogical view is held by a set of individuals who confuse poverty with humility. Syl, a well educated young man (with a Bachelor's Degree in Geology), was an ardent apostle of this school of thought; and he had vowed never to marry any girl whose parents were rich in terms of material wealth.

His father was much more excited at the mention of Innocent Osuagbara as the father of the young girl whom Syl had chosen for a wife. When they were at Saint Theresa Grammar School, they were close friends; and If eventually their children got married to each other, their long-time relationship would be revitalized and further cemented.

Papa Syl had already begun to imagine how he would be going to Umuike, to Serah's house. If he got there, he would ask Mama Serah to bring the leftover food from the previous day's supper. If she did, he would sit at the dining table with Papa Serah, each facing the other, chatting as they enjoyed the meal.

After eating, Papa Serah would bring out some special drink - local gin or palm wine would use to wash down the food. In the end, Papa Syl would mount his bicycle and go back home. If his wife asked him where he had been, he would proudly tell her he had been at his in-laws' place and had enjoyed himself to the fullest.

When his second son was getting married, he had advised him to marry from a neighbouring village so that he could have where he would be spending his leisure time. Unfortunately, the young man wouldn't listen to him and went ahead to marry an Iduu-na-Oba girl, the home of whose parents was unknown to Papa Syl.

The joy of having a second daughter-in-law soon was however short-lived, as his dream for a more cemented relationship with his former schoolmate, Innocent, was soon aborted.

On Sunday, Syl went back to the city. On the following day, at about 3:30 pm, as the intensity of the sun reduced, his father brought out his white bicycle (White Horse as it was commonly called) and after dressing up, mounted the bicycle and made his way down to Umuike. He wasn't going to Innocent's house, but to one of his aunties who was living in the same village. Nnenna was the name of the woman and she got married to an indigene of Umuike village about fifty years back. She was stocking her wares in a metal basin to go to the evening market when her eyes strayed away; and behold, she saw a wild rabbit in broad daylight!

"This person looks like Livinus,' she muttered, looking fixedly at the approaching figure. Soon, Papa Syl arrived and got down from his bicycle.

'Livinus!' Nnenna called him staring at him suspiciously.

'Daanta!' Papa Syl called her. "Who brought you to my house? I hope all is well?' She asked him still staring at him.

'Daanta, how could you say that?' he questioned and added: 'Haven't I been coming to your house before?'

'To whose house have you been coming?' she retorted and at the same time waved him to a seat. 'Now, tell me when last you came to my house.'

'When Daanta Ego died, didn't you see me here? he asked, now sitting on a bench.

'Does that one count?" she asked. 'You came for something else, but merely stopped by.'

'Daanta, it counts,' he argued.

'It doesn't,' she said. 'It does,' he insisted.

'Okay, apart from that one, which other time have you come?' she asked.

Papa Syl kept mute.

"That's why I told you that you don't come,' Nnenna

boldly said and then added: 'If you want to go to someone's house, you decide from home you're going to that person's house, just the way you've done today.' 'Okay, I've come today. Go and bring all what you have for me,' Papa Syl teased her.

'It's true-o! What am I going to offer you for kola?" Nnenna asked rhetorically as she stood up to go into the house.

'Don't you have goats?' Papa Syl raised his voice and asked her jokingly. 'Why not give me one or slaughter one for me?'

'Nna m, its true-o!' Nnenna, responded from the room, goat. and also added: "You deserve more than one She had kept a kola-nut in her handbag; but when she searched for it, she couldn't find it.

'Nna m, it's the kola-nut I kept in my handbag that I've been searching for,' she said to Papa Syl as she came out.

Papa Syl laughed telling her not to bother herself about kola.

'Am I so much of a guest that you should worry about offering me kola?' he asked her.

'Why not?' Nnenna said, 'especially for somebody that has come all the way from Amata.'

'Daanta, please stop worrying about kola,' Papa Syl said. 'Okay', she said, 'let me owe you a debt of kola nut'.

'Alright, that's okay by me, for there's something very important for which I came,' responded Papa Syl.

'Didn't I say it, that for this your broad daylight visit, something must be wrong,' Nnenna said.

'Daanta, nothing is wrong, just that I want to find out something from you,' Papa Syl said.

'Would you please sit down and let's talk.'
'Nna m, are you sure you're telling me the truth?' Nnenna asked, palpitating.

'There's no problem,' Papa Syl assured her.
'Nna m, did you say there's no problem?'
'Daanta, there's no problem.'
'True?'

'I'm the one telling you: there's no problem,' Papa Syl reassured her.

'Ngwanu, since you say there's no problem, let me believe you. I trust, you won't tell me lies,' she said and then sat down; though she still had a speck of doubt lingering in her mind.

'Daanta, the reason why I came is this..." Papa Syl said in a hushed voice, ..there's a young girl my son told me he saw in this your village. So, I decided to come and see you and also ask you, as my own person, if there's something you can say about her, because our people say that it is he that is sitting closer to someone that perceives the odour of his mouth.

"That's why I've come. Thank you.' he raised his voice and said.

Nnenna heaved in relief without even replying to the 'thank you'. Since Papa Syl came she had been kept in great suspense, as to whether he had brought some bad news, probably one of some death in her paternal home.

'I'm now relieved,' she confessed. 'Otherwise, I've been thinking that someone died and that you came to inform me about it,' she added.

'Daanta, does it mean I'm now a vulture that appears only when somebody dies?' Papa Syl asked and went into a hysterical laughter.

'No, Nna m, just that you're not used to coming to my house and so I thought that as you came today, perhaps something bad has happened,' Nnenna said.

'No, Daanta, it's just about what I've told you,' Papa Syl said.

'It's okay,' Nnenna said. "Which of my brothers saw the young girl?' she further asked.

'It's the eldest one,' Papa Syl said.

'Oh! Is he grown up enough to get married?' Nnenna asked, surprised.

'Of course, yes!' Papa Syl said. 'Even, the one after him is married for the past three years.'

'Really?' Nnenna asked with an air of surprise. 'Yes, of course!' Papa Syl responded.

"Thank God!' Nnenna said. 'Who did he say is the father of the young girl?' she further asked.

'According to him, she's the daughter of Innocent,' Papa Syl said.

'We've two Innocents in this our area; which of them are you talking about?'

'It's Innocent Osuagbara, the one whose father was once a palm oil producer.'

'Okay, but he has, altogether, three girls,' Nnenna said. 'Which of his daughters is that?' she asked. 'The one they call Serah,' Papa Syl said.

'Oh! Serah, our darling girl!' Nnenna said and then added: "The girl is pretty and has a good character. In fact, she is ranked as one of the best behaved girls in this village'

'So, you're assuring me, she has a very good character?' Papa Syl asked. 'Yes; but that notwithstanding, if your son intends.to marry her; count me out as intermediary or guarantor,' Nnenna said.

'Daanta, are they outcastes?' Papa Syl asked in a very hushed tone, his voice dropping to a muffled whisper.

'Nnaa, I've not said so. All I've said is that if and whenever you people are coming, I'll not stand as a surety,' she repeated bluntly, adding: 'You may now use your tongue to count your teeth?

Papa Syl kept silent nodding like the red-headed male lizard. He didn't know that Innocent's family had any kind of blot. When they were in school, he had always seen him as having no socio-cultural stigma, just like he himself; and they were friends.

Certainly, he was very much perturbed. In the first place, his dreams of having a cemented relationship with Papa Serah had come to an end. Moreover, he was afraid Syl might not think of getting married in the next five years. When next would Syl see a girl that would, for him, be as qualified as Serah was?

Serah was not only poor, she was also dark and rather tall: what one would describe as a "black beauty".

But come to think of it, why this unfortunate obnoxious cultural practice which prevents people from marrying whom they desire to marry? In fact, left to Syl and his father alone, they would have forged ahead with the marriage, but for what people would say. Moreover, if they dared insist on marrying Serah, none of their family members would agree to go with them; and in Igbo land, one does not marry without the cooperation and support of one's family and kinsmen.

'Daanta, I've heard what you said,' Papa Syl suddenly said.

'Ngwanu, Nna m, that's how it is. You know our people say that a fowl with a deformed leg is never sold nearer home. There's no way I'll see something that's not good and allow you to take it,' Nnenna said.

'That's the reason why I first came to you,' Papa Syl said. 'I knew that however it is, you must tell me.'

'Why not!' Nnenna exclaimed. 'Aren't you my.own person?' "That's it,' Papa Syl said. 'Daanta, let me be on my way home."

'Ngwanu, nna m, let me owe you a debt of kola which I promise to pay when you come next time' Nnenna said standing up at the same time as Papa Syl.

'No problem,' Papa Syl said.

'Ngwanu, go well.'

'Alright!'

'Greet our people." 'Okay!' Papa Syl said as he mounted his bicycle.

Chapter Two

In less than one year, Syl met another girl called Patricia. Just like Serah, Patricia was black, beautiful and of poor parentage. The clear distinctions between the two were that, whereas Patricia was from Umunze village, Serah was from Umuike and whereas Serah was an osu (outcaste), Patricia was diala (freeborn).

When Syl told his mother about Patricia, she was infuriated. According to Mama Syl, Umunze people were very bad and so her son would not marry from there.

On the other hand, his father, Livinus, had no qualms about his choice of Patricia for a wife. Papa Syl was the kind of person who believed that something good can come from anywhere. When he heard of his wife's resistance, he summoned her to his bedroom and issued her a subtle warning such that on the day they went for introduction, Mama Syl didn't have any other choice than to go with them.

The introduction was on a Wednesday, Afo market day, according to the Igbo calendar. At about 2:30 pm, Syl, his parents and Eme, a member of their extended family, went to Umunze with a keg of palm wine. When they got to Patricia's house, Mama Syl was much more disappointed. This time, it was no longer because her son went to the wrong village, but because he went to the wrong family. As soon as Papa Patricia saw them, he sent for his family members; and no sooner had the visitors taken their seats than the five elderly men arrived. The visitors were then offered kola which was presented by Maazi Oluigbo, Patricia's eldest uncle, who also said a brief prayer over the kola.

After eating the kola, the drink brought by Syl and his people was brought out and kept on a table before both villages.

'We have seen your drink,' said Maazi Oluigbo, 'but we don't know yet what it's all about. Please, would you tell us?"

At that point, Maazi Eme stood on his feet and bellowed greetings to both his people and their prospective in-laws.

'My in-laws, may you live long,' he said to the Umunze people.
'May you live long, too,' the Umunze people responded. 'My people, may you also live long,' he said also to Syl and his parents.

'And you, too,' they responded.

Maazi Eme cleared his throat and then continued. "There was a very beautiful chicken we saw on the road. As we watched and admired it, it entered this compound. That's why we're here, to see whether we can take a closer look at it.

'May you all live long,' he concluded, and then sat down.

'And you too,' both villages responded in unison.

Then, there was an interlude of silence; but soon, it was broken by a response made by Maazi Oluigbo, as the elder spokesperson of the host family.

'We've heard what you said,' Maazi Oluigbo said, 'but, as we all know, one does not jump across a trench upon the sound of a single gunshot. I hope you all understood what I mean?'

'Why not!' Papa Syl and Maazi Eme said. 'Aren't we all full-blooded Igbos?'

Although Syl could not unscramble the import of the adage, it didn't matter much, since his father and his uncle did. As far as that mission was concerned, they were his eyes and ears as well as his mouth. Whatever decision they took or agreement they entered into on that mission, was binding on him.

The introduction took place in the obi (a thatched shed in front of Papa Patricia's house.) Thereafter, Syl and his people were taken into the house and offered some food and drink which Patricia's parents had prepared for them. Meanwhile, Patricia's people stayed back in the obi helping themselves to the palm wine brought by Syl and his people.

Mama Syl refused to eat; and as her people helped themselves to the delicious meal of akpu and egusi soup, she was busy exploring the entire room where they were being served. She looked from the thatched roof of the room to the unpaved floor. She imagined how Syl, her son "Chukwudi", could bring his friends to such a humble, dilapidated environment and tell them it was the place he married from. Wouldn't they spit at him and call him all sorts of derogatory names? A whole "Chukwudi" of all people!

As all these things were still going on in her mind. her people finished eating. By then, Patricia's people had finished the palm wine in the gallon. Syl and his people picked up their empty gallon and went home.

On Saturday, they came back carrying two kegs of palm wine, some cartons of beer and crates of malt drink. This time, more people were involved. As usual, Papa Patricia informed his people and they gathered to enjoy the drinks. In the end, Syl and his people were asked to go back home so that both families could investigate each other's background to see whether there was any reason why Patricia and Syl should not get married to each other, although both families knew themselves very well as having no cultural encumbrances.

Papa Syl had earlier gone to Patricia's village and obtained all necessary information as regards the latter's family background. The person he met was his colleague in P&T (Posts and Telegraph). The man's name was Kelvin Otuonye, but Papa Syl called him K.O. He gave him a rundown of Patricia's family background, and even added that they were all related. 'His father shares the same grandfather with my. father,' Kelvin told Papa Syl referring to Patricia's father. On the other hand, Syl's family was very popular in the entire town such that no one could think of it as having any cultural stigma.

On Monday, Papa Patricia sent a message to Amata requesting Syl and his people to continue coming. The next day was Eke market day and so they couldn't go. It was a taboo in their land to marry on Eke days. They thus postponed it to Wednesday which was Orie.

On that day, Patricia had to let her people know who her husband was. After the guests were offered kola, a native cup, called okuku, was filled with palm wine and given to Patricia by her father, with the following instruction:

'Give it to whoever you want to be your husband.' She carried the drink to Syl and knelt down before him. Syl took the cup from her; and after draining i handed it back to her, together with some mone She went back to her father and returned the cup, a well as

hand over to him the accompanying
money.
Her people thus realized the particular
person the had come to marry her out
of the total number of fou men that
had come from Amata. Otherwise,
some c them might have been thinking
it was Mazi Oluigb or one middle-aged
man who was in their company Girls of
these days can create a dramatic
scene as an of them could decide to
marry a man as old as he father, if the
man happens to have plenty of
money.
Before Syl and his people went back
home, a lis for the four-day marriage
was issued to them; and a they went
home, they took Patricia along with
them.

In the night, Patricia slept in the same room wit Mama Syl. At midnight, the latter woke up to monito how Patricia slept. Mama Syl checked whether sh snored and whether she slept with her lips parted Another thing she checked on Patricia was whethe she talked while asleep.

In the morning, Patricia took a broom and swept everywhere in the premises, including the adjoining compounds. Next, she washed all the plates in the house and finally, she prepared the breakfast. She made sure everyone in the house that morning (including their neighbours who came to see the 'new wife') was served the food before she could think of herself. As she had her own breakfast, everyone watched her to see how she ate.

The breakfast was bread and tea. In the afternoon, Papa Syl went into his yam barn and brought out some tubers of yam. Mama Syl had some dried fish in her ngiga. She brought out some of the fish and gave to Patricia. With those things, Patricia prepared yam pepper-soup. As usual, she served everyone before she ate her own.

In the evening, Syl showed her round the village. They began with their immediate neighbours. If they came to any house, the people therein would tell her not to reject them.

'Nne, please, agree to marry us, okay?' they would tell her.

'Okay!' Patricia would reply nodding her head.
In the end, the family would offer them kola and some other gifts.

When they came back home, she had to prepare the dinner, although she cooked only the fufu. Mama Syl never allowed anybody to cook soup for her, more specially whenever her son, Chukwudi, was around Earlier, she had gone to the local market and purchased me soup ingredients: anara leaf, ugba and ogiri as ell as some periwinkles. Before she came back from market, Uloma, her younger sister's daughter who _s staying with her had pounded the other soup redients for her. As soon as she came back, she nt straight into the brick kitchen and prepared the cious vegetable soup. By then, it was already dark. cia, as usual, served everyone before she retired room where she enjoyed her own meal with Syl n Friday, Mama Syl went to a distant market to ase most of the items spelt out on the four-day age list. The ones she didn't buy, such as firewood, etc, were the things they could arrange at home. On Saturday, they took those items to Umunze. Syl did not go with them. He had earlier gone back to the city. He had a very crucial appointment to keep in the city. One of his colleagues in the office was doing her wedding on that day and he had a very important role to play at the occasion.

The person that led the mission was Syl's father. Just a few other men were also part of the delegation, but majority of the people involved were women, including Patricia who carried the palm wine on her head as they went. As soon as they arrived, Mama Patricia sounded the female gong (ogene ndi-inyom). It is a metal instrument that has a hollow oval cross section shape. Soon, all the Umunze women at home gathered. By then, the guests had taken their seats; and soon they were offered kola. The kola was a blend of oji (kola-nuts) and some afufa (giant garden eggs), two plates of okwa-ura (peppered meat snacks) and a keg of palm wine.

After the eating of kola, Mama Syl and her fellow women retired to the backyard where they sat down with the Umunze women to check the

things they had brought against the list
that had been given them Umunze
women had a secretary called Calista
who was saddled with the
responsibility of giving out the lists.
She opened her big register; and as
she called the items one by one, her
fellow women cross-checked them
with what were brought by the Amata
women.

On the list were four tubers of yam,
four lengths of bar soap, four heads of
dried tobacco leaves and four kegs of
palm wine. Other things were a bundle
of firewood tied with a piece of jorji
cloth, a bag of salt, two bottles of
pomade, one bottle of snuff, four
coconuts, one leg of goat meat and
physical cash of twenty thousand
naira. All the things were complete;

and they belonged exclusively to Mama Patricia.

As the Amata women collected the four-day marriage list on Wednesday, they had also issued their own list of what Mama Patricia would offer them on the appointed day. On the list were a cooler of fufu with its special soup to be prepared with a big fish, a tray of rice containing some pieces of meat and a leg of goat meat which was to be taken home, to prove to those who couldn't come that their mission was successful and that they were well entertained by their inlaws.

As they went home that night, the Amata women took along with them another list of items for the eight day marriage. Everything on this list was double what was on the four-day marriage list; and these were to be shared between Mama Patricia and her fellow women, the former taking the lion's share.

Few days after Patricia returned from the eight-day marriage, her people (including the youths) accompanied her to her marital home to know where their daughter and sister was being married. Her mother had prepared a pot of akidi (native beans) and some agbaratii (peppered egusi snacks); and had purchased a reasonable quantity of kola-nuts. As they went to Amata that afternoon, she carried those things. The kola-nuts and the agbaratii were to be given to Syl's father and the native beans, to his mother.

After they had been offered kola, Syl
was called up; and he began to dish
out physical cash to them. Some
people received higher than others,
depending on each person's
relationship with Patricia. For instance
Patricia's father got ten thousand
naira, her mother received five
thousand naira whereas another
woman who was just a member of
Patricia's family received two
thousand, five hundred naira, etc.

All the money given to them by Syl
was called "The-ihi-n'afo" as that was
the first time Patricia's parents and
kinsfolk were to eat in their new inlaw's
home. This was followed by their
being treated to a lot of food and
drinks. Before they arrived, Mama Syl,

assisted by her fellow women and a few young girls who either shared the same extended family with them or were her most desirable in the village, had finished cooking; and all the drinks meant for the event were ready. Earlier, Syl had driven down to the junction where he purchased some crates of beer and assorted soft drinks. Much earlier, Isaac, the palm wine tapper, had delivered five kegs of palm wine for which Syl had paid him in advance.

Some women had come with cellophane bags and empty water bottles; and as they got their own shares. they put them in those containers. The cellophane bags were for rice and other solid foods while the bottles were for drinks, more especially the soft drinks for their little ones who couldn't come with them.

Patricia didn't go back with them. She had to spent another sixteen days at Amata before she could visit her father's house again. This represented the sixteen day marriage in the Igbo marriage custom.

Syl wasn't around when his father collected the list for the kinsmen's rights. When he came back at the weekend, the two of them went together to Umunze and gave Papa Patricia the distinct sum of sixty thousand naira. This money, called "Ego-Chere-M" would be used to host them whenever they would be coming to deliver the kinsmen's rights; and the day mutually agreed on for this

fabulous event was the upper
Saturday.

On the list were sixteen kegs of palm
wine, eight crates of Star beer, four
crates of Maltina, four packs of
cigarette, one bottle of snuff and four
heads of dried tobacco leaves as well
as some large pieces of potash with
which to grind the tobacco into snuff.
Above all these was a fat goat called
"Ewu-Onuaku"; to be shared between
Papa Patricia and his family members.
Apart from these items, the sum of
forty thousand

naira was paid. Out of this money, ten
thousand belonged to Umunze
Progressive Union and five thousand
for all the kinsmen who took part in the
bride-price ceremony, while Papa

Patricia was entitled to the remaining sum of twenty-five thousand naira.

Culture, simply defined, is a practice or habit that over time becomes a way of life of a people. Over the years, the Igbo (as a distinct people of the sub-Saharan Africa) have evolved a sophisticated culture. One of these cultural practices is the payment of "bride price" to enable a man exercise full right over a woman he calls his wife.

After settling the kinsmen, the bride price was negotiated. Papa Patricia demanded fifty thousand naira while Papa Syl, on behalf of his son, offered to pay thirty thousand naira. In the end, they agreed on forty thousand naira. Syl counted the money and gave it to his father who in turn gave it to Papa Patricia Out of the total money, Papa Patricia took just five thousand naira only and gave the rest back to Papa Syl saying: 'I didn't mean to sell my daughter to you'. He would have given the whole money back, but for the fact that it would have given the wrong impression that he regarded his daughter as a nuisance he was anxious to let go without asking for anything in return.

When Syl and his people were going home, they were given a pot of akidi which they carried home and Patricia went home with them.

As dry season drew near (precisely in the month of October) Patricia's parents, Geoffrey and his wife, went to

Amata to secure the banns of marriage for their daughter. When they got to Saint Charles Catholic Parish, Amata, the Parish Catechist was sitting behind a writing desk in the office porch, while he attended to people that came to book masses and for other minor cases. The Parish Priest himself was inside his office, behind closed doors, dealing with more serious cases like family problems and issuance of marriage banns. Mr and Mrs Geoffrey Odunze took their seats In the porch waiting for their turn to go and consult with the Parish Priest.

Papa Syl was also at the parish house. He came even earlier than Geoffrey and his wife. Mama Syl didn't come. She was at home preparing something for her son's parents-in-law,

Mr & Mrs Odunze. Papa Syl had gone to a big market on the previous day and purchased a very fat fowl; and before he left home that morning for the parish office, he had slaughtered the fowl, butchered and handed it over to his wife who would use it to prepare an egusi soup. The plan was that, when Patricia's parents finished from the office, they would be invited over by Syl's father to help themselves to the delicious meal before going back to Umunze.

Soon, it was their turn to see the parish priest. The parish priest rang the table bell inviting them in. The priest was in suitane, sitting behind a writing desk. The desk was covered with a white cloth and on top of it was

a small table bell, assorted types
books as well as a crucifix.

'Mr Ohaka!' the priest called as he
raised his eyes up and saw Papa Syl.

'Good morning, Father,' Papa Syl
greeted him. 'Morning,' he responded.
'Who're the people with you; your in-
laws?'

'Yes, Father,' Papa Syl replied.

'Are you marrying theirs or are they
marrying yours?'

'I'm marrying theirs."

'Brother and Sister, you're welcome,'
the priest said to the couple.

"Thank you, Father,' they responded.

'Your names; and where are you people from?" the priest asked them.

'We're Mr and Mrs Geoffrey Odunze from Saint Theresa Parish, Geoffrey said.

'Oh! From our neighbouring parish!'

'Yes, Father."

'You're most welcome.'

'Thank you, Father.'

"Yes? Mr Ohaka, what can I do for you?' The priest gestured to Papa Syl.

'Father, my son wants to wed. So, we've come to obtain banns for him,' Papa Syl said.

'Ok,' said the Priest, 'but, Mr Ohaka, are you sure I know that your son?' he further asked.

'Well, Father, I can't say I'm sure. All I know is that he worships here whenever he comes home," Papa Syl said.

'If, in truth, he worships here, all this while we've been doing "Oru gaba" and "Support the Parish" have I ever seen him put any money?'

'Father, he might have been putting some money but you know it's not everybody who puts money that you see.'

'Who's that person that puts money in this church that I don't know? Mr Ohaka, so, your son is one of those people that shy away from church projects?! even heard that he works in an oil company; yet, he can't come here and make some donation to us. Ngwanu, it has set; let him go to that place he donates money and obtain the marriage banns.'

Papa Syl caught cold instantly as he noticed that the focus had shifted. They were no longer talking of the banns of marriage. The issue now was money which Syl had not been giving to the church. Before anything, he needed to pay all his "arrears" to the church; otherwise, no banns for him!

'Father, please he's not at home. Whenever he returns, I'll tell him...,' Papa Syl pleaded. 'Where is he?' the priest asked.

'He's in the city where he works,' Papa Syl replied, almost weeping. 'Go and bring him,' the priest said with an air of finality.

Before Papa Syl could say any other thing, the Priest had rung the bell inviting other people into the office. Meanwhile, the Odunze couple were confused. They couldn't imagine that sort of "embarrassment" as they perceived it.

'How could a priest do such a thing to us?' they wondered in their mind without saying it out. 'He didn't say the young man isn't paying his yearly contribution (YC), rather that he's not making donations to the church: donation for that matter!' It all seemed incredible; but it was real.

Papa Syl sent a message quickly across to his son. Under one week, Syl came home. He went immediately to the parish house, made his own donation and cleared all his outstanding financial debts to the parish, as well as the accompanying fine for late payment. His name was thus entered in the big register.

Two envelopes were issued to him. One was to be taken to Saint Theresa

Parish while the other, to Saint Mary
Catholic Parish, where he worshipped
in the city, so that as the banns were
being announced in Saint Charles,
they were, so also being announced in
the other two parishes.

On the following Sunday, the banns
were read for the first time in Saint
Charles Catholic Church. Those who
knew Syl were very happy to hear his
name called for wedding. After mass,
some of the women met his mother to
congratulate her.

'I heard nnaa's name in the church,'
they told her, referring to Syl.

'Yes,' she replied.
'Thank God,' they said and then left.

The banns were announced successively for three Sundays. When Syl went to collect it, the parish priest referred him to the Catholic Youth Organization (CYO) of the parish for clearance. He went to the youth leader; but when the CYO register was opened, it was discovered that his name was not there.

Eventually, they charged him a whooping sum of fifteen thousand naira before he could be registered and issued a clearance note.

The same process was undergone at Saint Theresa Parish. The banns were announced for three consecutive Sundays. In the end, Patricia was cleared by the parish Mary League of St Theresa Parish Umunze. She was an active member of the society and so spent far less than Syl.

Before their wedding, they underwent a compulsory three-month marriage course. Patricia did her own in the village while Syl did his where he was living in the city; but they had to do it together for the last week before the wedding day.

Chapter Three

Gongogom,...gongogom,... sounded the female gong in the early hours of Saturday morning. Almost immediately, all the women of Amata village assembled at the village hall. It was at the request of Mama Syl that the gong summoned the women; and so, she had to bring some kola to the hall.

The kola was the native garden eggs, wrapped with cocoyam leaves. She gave it to the woman leader (chairlady) who in turn presented it to the entire women.

"This kola I'm holding here was brought by Aunty Livina,' she said, holding the kola up in her right hand, *and she has asked me to tell you that her son will be wedding soon.'

'Oh, is it time already for the wedding?' the women murmured among themselves.

'When is it coming up?' a voice asked.

'On the 15th of this month,' Mama Syl answered. 'Where is it taking place?' another voice asked.

'It'll take place where they're living,' Mama Syl said "Where are they living?' another voice asked. and Mama Syl also told them.

"Then you will give us our rights at home,' the second voice said.

'Of course, I know,' Mama Syl responded. 'But will it be before or after the wedding?'

'Before the wedding of course', many a voice answered simultaneously.

"Then, when would you like to come for it?' Mama Syl asked.

Some suggested the fifth of that month. Others suggested tenth, but Mama Syl opted for the twelfth as most convinient for her. She would have to go to a big market to buy most of the things that would be needed.

On the eleventh, she went to the market and bought two baskets of processed but uncooked cassava, one big dried fish, some quantity of red meat, tomatoes, egusi and other soup and stew ingredients. She did not buy rice since she already had a bag of rice in her food store. Later in the day, she went to Imelda, one of her neighbours, and requested her to come and help her cook the food on the following day. Imelda assured her that she would come provided they would finish the cooking before ten o'clock in the morning when she would be going for a burial.

'Of course, we will," said Mama Syl. 'What are we going to cook that will take that long? It's only akpu and stew. After cooking those two, you'll be done. I'll prepare the soup myself and take care of the rest.'

'No problem then,' said Imelda while Mama Syl thanked her for accepting to help.

Very early in the morning, Imelda came in for the cooking. Before then, Mama Syl had begun to cook the akpu. She had made the fire and placed on it a big iron pot with some water in it. Now, she was softening the cassava with water while waiting for the water to start to boil. Imelda took over the work from her; and when the water started to boil, she moulded the cassava into balls and put them into the pot.
Meanwhile, Uloma was pounding the egusi in a small mortar. Mama Syl did not like grinding egusi with a grinding machine. According to her, egusi ground with a machine does not make soup thick. She herselfs was plucking the ugu vegetable and washing it in a big bowl of

water. When the cassava had boiled for about fifteen minutes on the fire, Imelda brought the balls out of the pot for the first pounding until they blended and became altogether soft and smooth. Then she moulded the half boiled fufu into balls again, put them back to the pot and allowed them to boil, while she did other things, until the cassava became due for the second and final pounding. By the time it was ten o'clock, the two women were done with all the necessary cooking, including the soup which Mama Syl would have cooked alone. Imelda then left for her house to prepare herself for her planned visit to her maiden village for a burial event.

Meanwhile, Mama Syl requested that the female gong be sounded again. It had been sounded the previous night to remind the women of their appointment. Soon, the Amata women began to drip into the Ohaka family compound, the venue for the event. Papa Syl had a very spacious obi roofed with metal roofing sheets and stacked with plastic chairs. Anyone that came went into the obi and waited for others to arrive.

When they had all gathered, Papa Syl went into the obi and offered them kola. In Igbo land, a woman does not present kola except in the absence of a man. Doing otherwise is considered a taboo. The kola consisted mainly of garden eggs with a few kola-nuts, presented in a tray.
After blessing and breaking the kola-nuts, Papa Syl took one whole kola-nut and handed the rest over to the woman-leader, who called on the provosts to do the sharing. Usually, the officers would take first before the floor members. Thus, the provosts carried the kola to the high

table, presenting it to the officers, one after the other. Some took lobes of kola-nut while others took garden eggs. However, there were those who took both kola-nut and garden egg.

When the officers had all taken, the remaining were split into smaller pieces and distributed to the floor members. The provosts then took theirs only after all the floor members had taken.
The stipulated rights of Amata women consisted of a cooler of rice, a cooler of fufu with its accompanying soup that contained one big fish and finally one crate each of malt and assorted soft drinks. After eating the kola, all these things were presented before the officers. They had, however, first contributed the money they would give to Syl on the wedding day before the food and drinks were brought out. As usual,

some of them came with cellophane bags and empty water bottles; and as they got their own shares, they put them in the containers to take home with them.

Before they left, they agreed on how they would attend the wedding. Each family group was to nominate a delegate. Nevertheless, much depended on the size of the vehicle which Syl was to provide for them: the bigger the vehicle, the higher the number of those that would attend the wedding, and vice versa.

The fourteen-seatter commuter bus arrived very late that Saturday morning. It had first gone to Umunze to pick Patricia's parents alongside other Umunze people, like the Mary League girls who were also going for the wedding. After Mr and Mrs Livinus entered the bus, only four chances were left. Already, over a dozen persons were waiting for the bus. Three of those people had come from Syl's maternal home and Mama Syl had insisted that all of them would for the wedding. Two out of the three were her elder brother and his wife. The other person was her father's younger brother who took care of them after the death of their parents. Therefore, there was no way she could ask them not to enter the vehicle. Papa Syl couldn't do that either.

When they eventually entered, only one chance was left. This sparked off criticism from Syl's kinsmen who were also invited to the wedding (with a crate of Star beer and a crate of Maltina). They had as well mapped out the sum of four thousand naira which they would give to

Syl when they got to the venue of the wedding reception.

"This is what Livinus normally does,' one of the men lambasted.

According to them, Papa Syl liked to "assault" (insult) them. The fellow that said this was Marcus. He wore white lace upon white canvas shoes.
'Na the same thing wey him do the other time we follow am go him friend burial.
He carry him in-law people full the motor,' Marcus raved.

They refused to attend the wedding and even dissuaded their "wives" from going. However, the women had already been given their own rights. So, they surreptitiously gave the money they contributed to Mama Syl who helped them present it to Syl.

It was past mid-day when they got to the
wedding reception venue. By then, the
wedding Mass was over. Other people
had represented both Syl's parents and
Patricia's parents: for Mr and Mrs Livinus
Ohaka, a couple from Amata who also
lived in the same city as Syl; and for
Patricia's parents, another couple whom
Syl had known in the city.

After series of photographs, Syl and
Patricia were driven home to their
residence by a friend. They had some
refreshment before going to the reception
venue.

The reception was in a hotel called
Queens' Palace located in the Mile Six
area of the city. It was a three storey
building painted pink, with cream colour
alumaco window frames and tinted glass

doors and windows. It had two reception halls, but Syl paid for the bigger hall which had the capacity of over three thousand seats. As soon as the couple arrived at the hotel, the MC was introduced by the spokesman of Syl's Committee of Friends.

The Committee of Friends comprised of ten young men who dressed corporately in black suit. No sooner had they introduced the MC than the latter began to call people to the high table. First, he called the chairman of the occasion who was the Human Resources Manager of the oil company where Syl worked. Next, he called the couple's sponsor and his wife. Then he called the parents of the just wedded couple: first, Syl's parents and then Particia's parents.

The last person the MC called to the high
table was Matthew, Syl's maternal uncle.
A village palm-fruit cutter, Matthew wore
a washed three-quarter combat jeans
with a t-shirt that had badges all over it,
and a face cap which had all together
made him look like an erstwhile guy-man.
His name was not on the list, but Syl told
his Bestman who went up and whispered
to the MC to include it. As soon as
Mathew heard his name called, he flew
from his seat and had nearly kissed the
floor while up rushing to take his seat at
the high table. Perhaps, he thought that if
he didn't hasten up, another person
might rob him of that elevated position.
After calling names to the high table, the
bride and groom were ushered into the
reception hall. Then a brief opening
prayer was said by a Reverend Father
before the chairman of the occasion
made his opening remarks.

Presentation of Kola was an important item on the programme of events, after which came the Cutting of Cake and then, the Bridal Dance. As the couple danced, people came out massively to spray money on them while the Committee of Friends picked the money. Some people who had higher denominations of currency notes such as five hundred naira denominations would go to them to request for change. Some of them would ask for fifty naira notes while others, twenty or even ten naira, depending on how much the persons had on them and also how much or for how long they intended to spray.

After the bridal dance, it was toast, Refreshment, Vote of Thanks from the bride and bridegroom, Presentation of Gifts and finally, Closing Prayers. On

Sunday, the couple went to church for thanksgiving. Two days later, they left for Uyo, Calabar and Obudu to spend their honeymoon.

Nine months after they came back from the honeymoon, it was obvious, looking at Patricia, that she would soon put to bed. Her belly was heavy and her two breasts bubbled like pumped balloons. Syl had earlier promised her a baby jeep if she would give birth to a baby boy. Against this background, she always prayed God to give her a baby boy. At times, she would visit the Blessed Sacrament and book Novena Masses, all to obtain the promise Syl made her.

He was on an official trip to Malaysia when Evelyn, their housemaid, called him on phone and told him that his wife had put to bed.

'What did she give birth to?' Syl asked.

'A baby girl,' replied Evelyn.
He didn't feel bad, but his joy came short
of what it would have been had Patricia
given birth to a baby boy. However, he
called his parents as well as Patricia's
parents to tell them what had happened.
Both parents were thrilled by the good
news, most especially Patricia's mother
who would tell virtually everyone that
came her way that her daughter had
given her a grandchild.

Unlike Syl's mother, the woman had not
had a grandchild even at her middle
sixties.

When he came back from Malaysia, Syl
travelled to the village so that they could
celebrate the new-born baby. As soon as

his village women saw him, they began to sing and dance for him, congratulating him on his wife's successful delivery. Though Syl didn't offer them anything there on the spot, he promised them that on the following day, they would all know the stuff he was made of: he would make sure they ate and drank to their satisfaction.

Later that day, he went to Umunze to see Patricia's parents. When the Umunze women saw him, they did exactly what the Amata women did: they sang and danced, calling him "Oke Ogo" (great in-law). Syl hastily gave som money to Papa Patricia who, immediately, arranged some crates of Malt and packets of biscuits. Everyone that came that evening enjoyed themselves to the brim nd had even gone home with a reasonable amount of money as Syl also doled out quite a few bundles of "cash".

When he came back from Umunze, he gave some money to his father to go and book for some kegs of palm wine for the forthcoming celebration. In the night, his father took a flash light and went to Isaac's house. He had just come back from work; and when Papa Syl came, he was taking his bath. Papa Syl couldn't wait for him to finish with the bath. He dropped him the massage while he was still in the bathroom.

'I would like you to reserve four gallons of palm wine for me tomorrow morning,' Papa Syl raised his voice and told him.

Isaac, responding from the bathroom, promised to do so; but to ascertain he didn't disappoint him, Papa Syl paid him right away for the drink. He handed the money to his wife who was cooking in the kitchen. The woman, in turn, gave it to one of her children who was giving her a helping hand in the kitchen. The little girl went quickly into the room, kept the money on the cupboard and returned to the kitchen to continue her bit.

The celebration took place in the morning. Later in the day (precisely in the evening), Syl and his father took the baby's dried and carefully preserved umbilical cord which the former had brought home with him from the city and buried it at the foot of a palm tree, right behind their family compound. That oil-palm tree later became known as "nkwu alulo Jessica" (Jessica's umbilical-cord palm tree).

Three months after the baby's birth, she
was taken to the church and baptized.
Her baptism name was Jessica while her
baptismal Godmother was Syl's
colleague in the oil company.

The baptism was on a Friday. On the
following Sunday, baby Jessica was
dedicated to God. Later in the day, there
was a reception party at Syl's residence.
The couple's relations and friends, as
well as their well-wishers, were all in
attendance to eat and drink and to
rejoice with the family. Syl surprised
everybody: not only his wife, but also all
who were present at the occasion.

As the ceremony was drawing to an end,
a Honda CRV with ribbons all over it
drove in. Syl took the microphone from
the MC. After a few words, he handed
the car's key over to Patricia. Rather than

burst out in excitement, Patricia burst into tears. How she wished she was God; she would have instantly reversed the baby's sex, in appreciation and profound gratitude to Syl for being such a darling husband.

She regretted not giving Syl a male child. However, Syl wiped her tears with his white handkerchief telling her that it wasn't her fault after all.

'My handsome husband,' she said to 'Syl, next time, I'll give you a baby boy, by the grace of God.' 'By His special grace, you'll do so,' Syl replied.

'And you'll buy me another car?'

'If you do so, I'll do twofold what I have done today."

'And you'll buy me beautiful cloths and shoes?' 'I'll do everything for you.'
'And take me out to Genesis?'

Syl didn't respond to the last question. He had realized that the car he bought for her was beginning to have some psychological effect on her. Everyone present also noticed it. They stared at her partly in admiration and partly with pity, crossing their arms on their chests while their heads tilted leftwards. Meanwhile, Syl took her to the privacy of their bedroom to pet her until she fell asleep.
By the time he came out of the room most of the guests had dispersed, having eaten and drank to their satisfaction.
Only a few very close friends waited patiently for more intimate chat and jokes before saying their byes.

Chapter Four

Syl employed a young man whose duty was, inter alia, to drive Patricia to wherever she wanted to go. If, for instance, she was going to the market, Etim would take her there and wait in the car until she finished buying whatever she wanted to buy. He would then drive her back home.

Today, the driver didn't come to work because one of his relations died and so he had to travel home for the burial. Patricia, having presumably graduated from a driving school and obtained a 'home-delivery' or arrangee' driver's license, could manage to drive herself, at least within the state metropolis. So, as she prepared to go out that Friday morning, in an attempt to play safe, she attached the L (learner) signs to both ends of the Honda CRV. Jessica was yet too tender to be left in the care of a maid; and Patricia's mother who came on baby-sitting visit had, after three months, gone back to the village. Therefore, Patricia tucked the baby up in a baby carrier and put her in the back seat of the car. She went over to the steering, turned on the ignition and, before she got to the gate, the gate-keeper had cleared the way for her. She drove out moving, at a snail's speed, as someone who had just learnt to drive. According to her, when she got to a road junction, she marched the accelerator instead of the break, and so ran into a truck that was carrying stone chippings. The car was squeezed up, and it took the concerted effort of the people around to open the doors. Patricia was seriously wounded, such that she didn't know when and how she was taken to hospital.

As the rescue team scrolled through her cell phone's book, they saw a number saved with "honey". When they called it, Syl was the person that picked it.

'Hurry up to the Rhohama Hospital,' they told him.

'Is anything the matter?' he asked. 'Just do as you're requested,' they said.

He abandoned all he was doing in the office (even without permission) and hurried off to the private hospital. When he got there, he was shocked at what he saw. His beautiful wife was in coma with open wounds all over her body. It is said that a man does not cry; but then, the expression of a strong and deeply-felt emotion is something that is not easy to suppress.

baby Syl fell down in tears beside the bed where Patricia was lying half dead. He cried like a but some hospital attendants consoled him with assurances that his wife would soon be okay.

After three days in the hospital, Patricia regained consciousness. "Where is my baby?" was her first question. Both Syl and the hospital attendants didn't know what reply to give to her. Would they tell her that Jessica was taking treatment? She would insist that they bring her, so that she could breastfeed her.

Unfortunately, the baby had died in the accident and when Patricia heard this, she shut her eyes and her breathing ceased. How could they be telling her this cock-and-bull story about her only baby, the only thing by which she could prove her womanhood to the world?

Syl rushed at her shouting aloud until she opened her eyes again. She insisted that Jessica's corpse be brought to her for her to see and ask the baby the reason why she chose to treat her mother so.

It took the rest of the day and the effort of over a million people to convince her that Jessica was not her destined child, and that God who gave her to her would still give her the right child that would come to stay.

For six months, Patricia received treatment at the Rhohama Medical Centre. When the open wounds were all healed, she was discharged and transferred to an orthopaedic hospital at the outskirts of the city. In the morning,

Syl would first visit the hospital to see how she was doing and to give her what he had for her, notwithstanding the fact that he had employed a lady to take care of her personal needs in the hospital. This invariably made him arrive the office very late. He would be very tired and would often sleep off on duty. Reports always got to the management of the company and from time to time he was summoned and cautioned against this unusual persistent lateness to work; but the love he had for Patricia was enormous and uppermost in his mind. Even when Fred, one of his colleagues, met him privately and told him about an unpleasant plan of their boss against him, he ignored him.

'Do you want my wife to die?' he asked Fred.

'It's not that I want your wife to die; but what I'm telling you is what I overheard our boss say,' Fred replied.

'Damn the boss! Damn his work!' Syl said as he walked out on Fred.

He had indeed been blinded by his love for Patricia forgetting that no matter how blind love may be, it is not unlikely that someday, the eyes will clear.

On one Monday morning, exactly a month after his meeting with Fred, Syl had gone to see his wife; as usual, before he went to work. He was so late that day that, soon after his arrival, an envelope was served on him. When he opened it, he discovered it was a letter from the company's management. He read the caption of the letter and couldn't believe what he saw. He robbed his eyes with his palms and revisited the caption; but the message remained unchanged. He then mustered courage and read through the body of the letter to see whether, in any way, there was a mistake somewhere: whether perchance the body of the letter was in disagreement with its caption.

Eventually, the unpalatable reality dawned on him that he had been fired, with immediate effect. Syl suddenly saw the morning sun, set. He could no longer remember his wife, her critical state of health and all the love he had for her. 'What is the meaning of love without a good job?' he was probably asking himself.

With the piece of paper in his hand, he rushed to the office of his boss. Although Mr Douglas felt sorry for him, he didn't give him any attention because he had warned him several times, but he wouldn't listen.

Syl tottered out of Mr Douglas' office and sat down on a pavement near the office, weeping out his eyes until some of his colleagues came and took him away.

After two years in the orthopaedic hospital, Patricia could now stand on her feet and walk. Syl thought it necessary to give her another pregnancy. Since Jessica died, their house had been feeling empty.

An even more compelling reason for impregnating her was the quest for a male child. In Igbo land, a man without a male child is considered incomplete, although he may have as many female children as possible. For the woman, she

is not yet sure of he marriage as her
husband could take up a second wife at
any time.

When the pregnancy turned five months,
Patricia was registered in a general
hospital for an antenata programme. The
programme was a weekly affair and
precisely on Tuesdays. Whenever she
was going for the programme, Syl would
offer her a lift with his car and from there
would go to the international airpor where
he now used his car for an airport taxi
service. Patricia would stay with her
fellow women who had also come for the
programme. and would take a public
transport to go back home.

After work, Syl would go into a big
market and buy foodstuff so that when he
got home he would not bother himself
with any neighbourhood street market

where those things are sold at relatively high prices.

Today, they wanted to eat garri and soup and so he had bought soup ingredients such as red meat dried fish and crayfish. He didn't buy red palm oil because Mama Patricia had brought them a 10-litre keg of red palm oil when she visited them last

The other things Syl bought were onugbu and egusi. He gave the egusi to a manual grinder to grind for him. When he got home, he found Patricia in their matrimonial bed staring at Jessica's pictures.

'Honey!' he called her; and when she turned, she looked pretty pale, as the anguish of her heart reflected boldly on her forehead.

'I thought I've warned you against watching these pictures?' he asked her taking the pictures away from her. She didn't talk; rather, she began to shed tears and Syl wiped her tears with his handkerchief.

'Let me get you what I bought for you,' he told her; and before he went down from the bed to get her the apples and oranges he bought for her, he gave her a peck.
Patricia refused to eat those fruits, no matter how hard Syl tried to persuade her. Syl later changed into another cloth and went into the kitchen to prepare the food.

The kitchen was very commodious and stacked with kitchen paraphernalia of sorts. Under normal circumstances, Syl would cook with the gas cylinder; but as there was no money to refill it, he managed the kerosene stove. First, he steamed the red meat alongside the dried fish. Next, he added the other soup ingredients: ground egusi, red oil, salt and finally the vegetable. When the soup was done, he brought it down from the fire and boiled some water with which he prepared the garri.

Before dishing out the food, he moped up the tiled floor of the kitchen and washed the utensils he had used in the cooking. Then he brought the food to the bedroom, only to discover that Patricia was still in anguish. He was pissed off. Yet, rather than scold her, he kept the food on the table and, as usual, climbed on the bed to pet her and persuade her that Jessica was not from God.

'If not, she wouldn't have died,' he said to her. However, Partricia, did not believe that there are some people who are not from God. Her Bible didn't tell her that during the creation of the universe, God created some people while the devil created others. Therefore, she didn't agree with her husband that Jessica was not from God. 'Or, even at that, why didn't she stay for me?" she asked.

In the circumstance, she refused to eat the food brought by Syl, no matter how much pressure the latter put on her.

As the pregnancy approached nine months, Patricia became very nervous, though they had gone for a scan and the scanning machine had shown that the baby in her womb was a male. 'Isn't it the same thing they said during Jessica's pregnancy; but in the end, I gave birth to a female child,' she said.

If she didn't give birth to a male child this time, Syl might decide to take up a second wife. His people had already begun to mutter about it.

Two years after the accident occurred, Mama Syl came to the city to see how her son, not Patricia, was doing. When she had spent three days in her son's residence, she decided to go to the orthopaedic hospital to see Patricia, 'just because of what people might say', as she told herself. 'Otherwise, I wouldn't have bothered myself going to see her. Isn't she the one that has kept my son in his present condition?'

That Saturday morning, as Syl was leaving for work. he first dropped her at the hospital so that she would stay with Patricia till evening when he would close from work and go and pick her up. When they came into the room where Patricia was, the latter was lying face-up in her sick bed.

'Patricia!' Mama Syl called emphatically while blinking her eyes maliciously.

Patricia didn't respond.

'My child, are you keeping mute to me? Am I the cause of your problem, eh, my child?' The woman asked with her palms thrown open.

'I wouldn't say so,' Patricia retorted, 'but no one has ever done what you have done."

'My child, what did I do? Or have I not been asking of you since this thing happened to you?' Mama Syl asked

'So, Mama, had it been I died in that accident, you wouldn't have been bothered! Papa, as well as every other member of the family, has come to see me; but you, my mother-in-law, who was supposed to be more worried about my condition, didn't come. Mama, if people had told me you would behave this way, I wouldn't have believed them. Anyway, no problem! After all, you are not my mother,' Patricia said with a trembling voice, tears gushing out of her eyes.

'My child, did you say I'm not your mother?' Mama Syl asked in anger.

'Yes, of course,' Patricia said boldly. 'If you were my biological mother and I had this accident since two years and some months now, wouldn't you have come to see me?'

All this while, Syl did not interrupt. He knew the whole truth of the matter; he knew that the reason why his mother did not bother to come and see Patricia since over two years the latter had the fatal motor accident and lost her only baby, was due to the fact that she (Mama Syl) was not in support of his marriage with her (Patricia) not necessarily because Patricia wasn't her biological child. However, he didn't say anything in the presence of Patricia. He wouldn't blame his mother in the presence of his wife, but of course, he had blamed her earlier at home.

He spent a few minutes with them before he entered his car and left for the airport.

After work, he came back to the hospital to see his wife and to pick his mother. As they went out of the hospital room, his mother began to tell him some of her observations vis-à-vis Patricia's state of health. According to Mama Syl, the accident affected Patricia's pelvic bone, and so she might not be able to give birth to a child again.

'Didn't I tell you Chukwudi, my son? I told you that Umunze people are very "problematic" but you wouldn't listen to me. Now, you're going to remarry. Of course, you're going to remarry! Otherwise, other people will inherit your property and turn round to laugh at you,' she said to Syl.

When Patricia overheard this, she closed her eyes very tight pretending she didn't hear it.

Very early on that Wednesday morning, at about 4:30am, as Syl was in a deep sleep, it seemed as if someone had touched him. He jumped up only to see Patricia sitting up in the bed and sobbing and with her left hand on her waist.

'Honey, what is it?' he asked her.

'My stomach,' she replied.

'How's it doing you?'

'It's as if the baby in my womb is moving about.' As soon as she said that, Syl understood what was

happening to her. He knew she was in labour and so began to pack some of her things in a bag. As he went out to reverse the car, he took the bag and put it in the car. When he came back to the house, he changed her cloth to something better and supported her to the car. Then, he went back and locked the house before they left for the hospital.

They went first to a maternity hospital, but were turned down by the owner. According to the midwife/ proprietress, Patricia did not register with them for her ante-natal care and so could not be delivered there. Then, they left for the General Hospital where Patricia did her pre-natal programme. Just a few kilometer to the hospital, the car began to give out a very naughty sound. In fact, since Syl bought it from Berger in Lagos, he had never seen it make tha kind of noise. He applied the break gently and the car slowed down gradually. Clearing to the roadside he pulled up and turned off the ignition. After a few seconds, he turned on the ignition again, but when he tried to drive off, the ugly sound got worse. He didn't bother himself opening the bonnet to know what was wrong with the car. He thought that doing so would be counter-productive as Patricia was becoming much more restless and might be delivered any moment from then.

He turned off the ignition again, went down from the car and stood by the road to hike for a taxi. Soon, a taxi came and he waved it down.

'General Hospital!' he said.

'One thousand!' replied the cab man.

'Oga, please, accept five hundred naira. My wife is on the verge of delivery. So, I'm taking her to the hospital,' Syl pleaded.

'Na me give your wife belle?' the cab man asked him. 'I beg if you no wan pay one thousand, make I de go my way. This na early morning.'

Inside his mind, he continued to say: 'You get mouth to tell me say your wife wan born. You don ask weda the one wey I marry for past ten years don born me any pikin? Please if you no wan go, make I commot.'

Syl declined to pay one thousand naira; but as the cab man tried to move, he stopped him. The two of them assisted Patricia into the back seat and Syl sat by her side supporting her with his body.

When they got to the hospital junction, the driver wheeled right and soon they got to the General Hospital. It was still a few minutes past 5am and so the hospital gate was supposedly still locked. However, their anxiety began when, after blasting the car horn for a long time, no one opened the gate for them. It was much later they realized that all the resident doctors in the state were on strike, because the state government owed them arrears of salary and allowances for more than five months.

The cab man threatened to discharge them at the hospital gate claiming his contract with Syl had expired; but Syl promised to pay him extra five hundred naira. He therefore reversed the car and took them to a private hospital called St Vincent Hospital.

By the time they got to St Vincent, there was daylight. The gateman opened the gate and they drove in. Syl supported Patricia out of the car; and with the help

of some nurses, he took her to the wait-
room before he came back and settled
the cab man who zoomed off
immediately after receiving the agreed
fare. From the wait-room, Patricia was
moved to the labour-room where vital
tests were conducted instantly:
temperature, blood pressure, weight,
blood group, haemoglobin etc. The chief
medical consultant of the hospital
complained that the baby in her womb
was so heavy she could not deliver it on
her own. Therefore, she was transferred
from the labour-room to the theater
where she underwent a two-hour surgical
operation.
Before surgery, however, Syl had make
deposit one hundred thousand naira.

after the birth Celine, Patricia became
delivered the baby through surgical
operation. had home get water flask.

When back to the hospital, theater. He asked her operation and

'Yes,' nurse, and congratulations for baby girl'

Immediately Syl heard it was female baby, he turned and went back home and never cared to see mother and child for close one month.

Consequently Patricia unilaterally named the baby "Nwanyibunwa" meaning that a child is a child be it female.

She was in the hospital for one month eating nothing else but food donated to her by her ward-mates. Syl had also refused to foot the hospital bill but for the eventual intervention of a friend of the family, their marriage sponsor, who also made it clear to him that a woman alone does not make a baby. 'According to medical experts, what you put into her, and especially the timing, determines what she gives birth to at childbirth,' Fidelis had told him.

Chapter Five

After footing the two heavy surgery bills, it became clear that Syl would no longer be able to pay for their bungalow apartment in the Government Reserved Area (GRA). Another even more pressing reason for that was the fact that the fault which the jeep developed was so complicated that even five hundred thousand naira could not rectify it. It was a case of gear box which might require ordering it from Japan before the car could be fixed.

Therefore, before their two-year lease expired, he offered the car for sale at a give-away price and used part of the proceeds to rent a two-room apartment in a low-cost area of the town. He then set up a foodstuff business for Patricia and used the remaining amount to buy a small car for a town-service taxi business.

The car was a Wagon Passat painted blue and white. Syl registered it in a park. In the morning, he would drive to the park and queue up for his turn to load. When it was his turn, they would load his car with five passengers (three at the back seats and two in the front seat). Out of the total sum of five hundred naira collected, he would give the park people fifty naira and drive his passengers to a place called Rumuorimili, a terminal point where he discharged all his passengers and immediately made a U-turn. Then, he would pick passengers along the way as he went back to the park. This was the practice everyday, except on Sundays, when he presumably rested, even as he often went for one meeting or the other, especially those of his village association or the local branch of his town's union.

Whenever he closed from work, he would drive down to a drinking spot called "Mama Chi-Chi". Mama Chi Chi was a fat, dark woman who traded in dry gin. Syl would always be at her road-side kiosk drinking and cracking jokes with his new-found friends and drinking mates till late in the night.

One day, as he had drunk himself into a state of stupor, either Mama Chi-Chi herself or one of her two daughters who helped her in the business, dipped hand into his pocket and collected all the money he made for the day.

'Oga Winter, wetin we go give you?' Mama Chi-Chi asked Syl when he arrived at the "joint". "Winter" was the nickname Syl assumed since he joined the taxi-driving work. He had once told his friends the origin of that name: When I dey young,' he said, 'I de play ball well well. Anytime I dey for any team, fear and serious cold go catch everybody wey dey for the other team. " Na him make my people come de call me "Winter." Once, when one little boy called him that name on their street, he immediately gave him one hundred naira in appreciation. In reply to Mama Chi-Chi's earlier question Syl (alias Winter) asked her 'You get monkey tail?'

'Yes,' the woman replied.

'Bring am,' he said.

She shook the transparent rubber bottle with some leaf and root particles inside it very vigorously, removed the crown on the bottle, filled a plastic cup to the brim and gave it to Syl.

Till 9:30 pm, Syl was sipping from the cup. When e had drained it, he gave Mama Chi-Chi one hundred naira, entered his car and drove home. When he got home, he didn't ask for food n did he ask his family if they had eaten anything

He simply took his bath and went to bed. In the morning, as he was preparing for work, his first daughter who was in Primary Two in a private school came to him to ask for her school fees.

'Good morning Dad,' the girl greeted him.

'Good morning', he responded and quickly followed it up with the question 'any problem?'

'Dad, our teacher said that we should bring our school fees today or we'll be sent out of the class, the girl replied.

'Go and tell your mother,' Syl said to the little girl.

'I've told her, but she said she doesn't have money,' Celine said with a tremble in her voice. 'Then, stay back at home,' he told the girl bluntly and walked out the room.

According to him, since Patricia had "refused" to give him a male child, she alone would take care of the two females she produced.

When he could no longer maintain the taxi cab, he sold it out to one of his fellow drivers called Alfonso. The man's real name was Alphonsus, but Syl reduced it to a diminutive for his own conven ience. At first, the man would pick offence when ever Syl called him by that name until one day, when the latter told him of Alfonso Anes who was a schoolmaster and also one of the foremost Bini converts to Christianity. From that day, Alphonsus began to enjoy the name, even puffing up each time Syl or any other person called him Alfonso.

Patricia and her two daughters came back from the market one Wednesday night. After cooking, they had their dinner, took their birth; but, until they went to bed, Syl had not come home. In the morning, she called their marriage sponsor on phone and told him what she was experiencing. Fidelis was not surprised at what Patricia told him. Syl had been keeping late nights, although, in fairness to him, he hardly ever spent a whole night feeloutside except on some rare occasions when they went for a funeral or some other social wake-keep.

Fidelis asked Patricia to calm her nerves till evening. If her husband didn't come back, then they would know what necessary steps to take. Patricia longer agreed with him and terminated the call; but she continued to feel restless. When she could no restrain herself, she moved down to the taxi park from where Syl operated. There she met one "Ala Owere", a tall slim dark man who was a driver in the park. She took him aside and asked him if he knew any driver called Sylvanus.

'How he be? Ala-Owere asked.

'He dey yellow and tall small,' Patricia said.

'And him de drive Wagon Passat?'

'Yes O!,' Patricia said.

'Oga Winter?' Ala-Owere asked.

'Na him!'

'I never see am for past three days,' Ala-Owere said and further asked: 'Na your husband be that?'

'Oga, na him be father of my pikin them,' Patricia said folding her arms on her breasts with her face thrown away.

Ala-Owere shook his head in disbelief, not necessarily because Syl was a disappointment but more because Patricia looked far much older than her husband, although she was just thirty-seven.

Why wouldn't she look so old: a woman that was always in the market, not only looking for what her children would eat, but also for what she would use to pay house rent and school fees?

In fact, as she was returning from the market one day in company with her two daughters after a torrential rainfall, she mistakenly stepped into a gutter covered with water and tumbled over into it.

The raging erosion carried her and was advancing rapidly towards a nearby river when her daughters raised an alarm. People responded promptly and rescued her.

I never see am for past three days,' Ala-Owere repeated, shaking his head.

'But when him de comot for house, he talk say him dey go work,' Patricia insisted.

I no see am here...' Ala-Owere said and then added: 'I even hear say he don sell him car." 'Which car?' Patricia exclaimed.

'Oh! He never tell you?' Ala-Owere asked.

'Oga, he no tell me - o,' Patricia said as she thre her palms open.

'Oga Winter!' Ala-Owere exclaimed with a chuckl 'After he don sell him car finish, where he come car money go?' he further asked, rhetorically.

'No be him girlfriend house?' Patricia said. 'I hear say he get girlfriend wey them de call "Baby Attraction" No be the woman house him carry all the money go?"

'Madam, you dey funny,' said Ala-Owere as he popped some laughter and asked: 'Which one be Baby Attraction?'

'Na laugh you de laugh so?' Patricia asked and added. 'Na wetin he tell him friend dem. Otherwise how I for know?'

Madam, leave wetin people de talk. Him no get da kind girl-friend.'

'Imagine wetin you de talk,' Patricia said. If I tell you say, since he de drive dat car, I never see him one kobo, you go believe me? Okay, if him no get dat kind girl-friend, tell me wetin de chop de whole money wey him de get. He no de pay house rent, as to say na wetin de chop him money. So, Oga, for every "them say" true word dey there'.

Ala-Owere then lost the nerves to engage in further argument with her. He had thought that Syl (alias Winter, as they knew him in the park) was responsible; but what Patricia had just told him had made him believe the saying that all that glitters is not gold.

'But you don call him number to know whether him number de go?' Ala-Owere managed to ask.

'Why not!' Patricia said and added: 'I bin de call am, but him don switch off him phone.'

'Anyway, only thing wey I fit tell you now be say, make you de call him number. Make you also de pray make God touch him mind so that, wherever he fit dey make him change mind and come back,' Ala-Owere said.

'Na him be de only thing,' Patricia concurred. 'Okay now...,' Ala-Owere said as he was about to go.

'Ok sir, thank you,' Patricia said, also taking her leave.

When, till the following day, Syl didn't return, his wife reported back to their marriage sponsor who advised her to see their village union's chairman.

Stephen was in his shop at Mile 3 market when Patricia came that afternoon reporting the incident to him. He quickly called a meeting of all their brethren residing in the city. In the evening, the Amata brethren gathered at his residence and he tabled the matter before them. One of them suggested immediately: "Let's bring the police into the matter". They all consented unanimously to the suggestion and two people (the union chairman inclusive) were delegated to contact the police.

On Monday, Patricia and the two men went to the police station and reported the matter. The police officer in charge of the command suggested that an announcement be placed on television declaring Syl missing. Patricia and the two men okayed the idea. Thus, the officer requested for and was given a good recent photograph of Syl for the Nigeria Television Authority.

Syl was watching the news that Wednesday night when his picture was displayed on the screen. He wasn't even bothered that he was declared missing. He simply smiled and

cleared his throat. 'When they are tired,
they'll relax,' he said.

Chapter Six

Phoebe (alias "Baby Attraction") would always go for shopping; and each time she did, Syl would dish out a huge amount of money to her.

When the money finished, she threw him out of her house. Syl was stranded; but he would not want to go back to his house. If he did, his wife would ask him where he kept his car. Would he tell her that he had sold it? If so, she would ask him where he kept the proceeds. What then would he tell her?

Of course, he would not tell her that the car was snatched from him by thieves; or else, she would ask him for how long and where he had been since then.

He roamed the city for three days, virtually on an empty stomach. On the fourth day, he decided to go back home, just like the Biblical prodigal son who, after squandering his father's wealth on women and drinks, decided to go back home. He picked up his "travelling bag" (a jute sack bag) from under the bridge and, in the evening breeze, he staggered home.

He got to number 824 Ikwere Street at about 6 pm. When his co-tenants saw him, they screamed, asking him where he had been for the past three months, but he didn't have any answer to give to them. He merely asked them about his family, in response to which he got the devastating information that they had packed out of the house.

Incidentally, as soon as Syl left, things became much more difficult for his family. Patricia was taking care of the two kids single-handedly and so, could not afford to pay for their two-room apartment as the due date for the next payment was fast approaching. Thus, before their rent expired, she quickly looked for a much cheaper one-room apartment. Meanwhile, she hired a mini truck and took some of their property to the village.

When their current rent expired, they packed into the new one-room apartment with the remaining property.

So, when Syl heard that his family had re-located, he felt much more stranded. The worst part of it all was that none of the neighbours knew where Patricia and her children had relocated to. In further desperation, Syl moved straight to Fidelis' house which was not far from number 824 Ikwere Street.

It was almost dark when he arrived at number 797 Ikwere Street. Fidelis had not come back from the market. The person he met at home was his wife, Fidelia. She was coming out of the kitchen carrying a cooking pot with two hands.

'Dee Sylva!' Fidelia shouted in utter surprise while staring at him.

'Yes!' he answered facing the earth rather than the woman.

'Where have you been since?' she asked him still staring at him; but he didn't talk. It is either he couldn't or wouldn't say a word.

Since almost four months now, you abandoned your wife and children. I hope you came back with your car?' she further asked him, but he still kept mute again.

'Are you keeping mute? I hope you have not sold that car?' Fidelia lashed out. 'They snatched it away from me,' Syl managed to say.

'They what!' she screamed and nearly threw the pot she was carrying to the ground. 'In short, you haven't said the truth yet about where you kept the car. When my husband, your godfather, comes back, you explain to him,' she said finally and went into the house to keep the pot. Meanwhile, she asked Syl to come in and sit down.

She was cooking rice and stew. When she finished cooking, she loaded a big dish and placed it on a table before Syl. Within the blink of an eye, he had demolished the food to the last grain. She asked him whether he was satisfied. Though he didn't say no, she knew from his reaction that he wasn't. Thus, she put more food for him. As he was battling with the second plate, he heard Fidelis' voice outside and was instantly pissed up.

'How will I face this man tonight?' he thought. What if he asks me where I've been for the past three months, what will I tell him? Will I begin to tell him all this trash I have been telling his wife?'

Incidentally, Fidelis was very intelligent and could not be deceived easily. Just as Syl thought about what to tell him, he opened the door and came in. 'Welcome!' his wife said to him sitting in one of the cushioned seats.

'Yes!' he answered. 'Who's this person with you?' he asked as his eyes strayed to where Syl was sitting. Syl himself had stopped eating as soon as he heard Fidelis' voice. He dropped his spoon in the rice plate and bent his head miserably over the table-top.

'Good evening, sir!' he greeted as he slightly raised his face up. Then, he put his eyes down again, 'Evening,' Fidelis responded, still not knowing who had greeted him. 'Fidelia, who did you say is with you?' he turned
to his wife and quizzed again.

'Get seated first,' Fidelia said to him.

When Fidelis took a seat next to his wife, he re-visited the question: "Who's with you?

'It's Dee Sylva,' she said.

'Which Sylva?' he retorted.

'How many Sylvas do you know? The one we sponsored in marriage, of course' Ohaka?' Fidelis asked.

'Sylva 'He says he is', replied his wife.

'Come, Sylva,' Fidelis turned and faced Syl squarely, 'where did you go to abandoning your wife and children for the past three months?' he asked.

Syl played the dumb again.

'Aren't you the one I'm asking?' Fidelis asked and repeated: 'Where have you been for the past three months?'

He still didn't talk. Instead, he began to sob like a child as if he was weeping.

'Has he seen his family?' Fidelis turned to his wife and asked.

'How could he have seen them? Does he know where they're living now?' Fidelia asked rhetorically.

'Of course, he doesn't,' Fidelis affirmed, 'because he had left before they relocated. Now, when you see them, you explain to them where you've been since three months.' he turned to Syl and said. 'What abou the car you left with? I hope you came back with it?

'Fidelia', he turned to his wife again, 'I hope he came back with that car?' he asked emphatically. 'Ask him,' Fidelia said.

Anyway, when you get back to your family, you'll explain to them,' Fidelis said, addressing Syl. "This time, you'll eat yourself. Of course, I trust Patricia. She will teach you the lesson of your life,' he said as he went to the bedroom to change his clothes.

After changing his clothes, he and Syl left his house. Fidelis led the way as they went to Isiokpo Street, where Patricia and her two daughters were now living. Syl was following behind him, carrying a jute sack bag like a little village boy returning home after his master had sent him away from the city.

When they got to the new yard at Isiokpo Street, it was already dark. Patricia and her children had just come back from the market.

'Kpom,...kpom,...kpom,... Fidelis said repeatedly while tapping his right palm against the left several times, waiting each time for a response from inside.

Incidentally, Patricia was by the side of the house arranging what they would cook, while her children had gone out to fetch water.
'Who's it? I'm coming-o!' she answered from where she was.

Soon, she came out carrying a kerosene lamp. 'Nne, I was wondering whether you and your children hadn't come back from market,' Fidelis said.

We're back,' she replied, even before she knew who the visitor was. Then as she raised the light up, to the visitor's face, she suddenly exclaimed: 'Oh! Dee Fide, are you the one?'

'Yes, I am,' Fidelis replied.

'Good evening, sir!' she greeted. 'We came back from the market just a short while ago,' she further added.

'Good evening,' he responded. 'What of the children? Where are they?' She told him where the two girls went to.

'Dee, come inside,' she requested him, opening the door while Fidelis removed his rubber slippers and followed her in; but when he looked back and discovered that Syl wasn't following him, he went out again only to see him perch on the wall, beside the entry door.

'Come inside now!' he said to him.

'Dee, who is in your company?' Patricia asked him. He laughed but didn't say a word yet.

Like Fidelis, Syl removed his pair of slippers also; and as he went into the room, he missed his steps and just managed to hold himself up from falling down.

'Good evening, sir!' Patricia greeted him without knowing yet whom she was greeting; but he didn't respond. Could it be because of the "sir" she added to the greeting? The title "Sir" is the exclusive reserve of responsible men, like the Knights, not a "woman wrapper" who had been serving a prostitute for the past three months, cooking for her and washing her underwears.

He simply fixed his gaze to the floor of the room. Patricia was overawed and at the same time more eager to know who Fidelis had brought to her house that wouldn't respond to greetings: whether it was a ghost or a human being that was in his company.

'Dee Fide, who did you say, came with you?' she asked Fidelis again.

'Nne, get seated first,' Fidelis said and added:
'come, Sylva, get seated as well.'

'Which Sylva?' Patricia retorted raising the light to confirm what she had heard: whether it was her husband or another person with the same name.

Eventually, she discovered it was the same man who abandoned her with her two daughters and went to God-knows-where.

'Papa Chiamaka, are you alive?' she asked Syl, who instantly began to shed crocodile tears; crocodile tears indeed he shed.

Meanwhile the following thoughts were going on in Patricia's mind 'Since he sold his car and had the proceeds with him, did he bother to come back until now that he is almost a corpse? He knows who is going to give him food, not Patricia. God forbid! Patricia that has been suffering to take care of the children! God forbid! Not me!' Then she managed to speak out to Syl: 'Since four months, you abandoned me and the children, where have you been?' Patricia asked wiping her tears with her wrapper. 'That's what I was also asking him,' Fidelis said.

'Dee Fide, where did he say he has been?' she asked Fidelis.

'He's here; ask him,' Fidelis said.

'Papa Chiamaka, where have you been since almost four months now?' she turned to Syl again and asked. He wouldn't want to talk; but when Patricia pressurized him, he wiped his tears and began to tell her the same cock-and-bull story he had earlier told Fidelis: how he was carrying a passenger to somewhere and along the way the young man brought out a pistol, showed it to him and asked him to clear to the roadside.

When he did, the young man pushed him out of the car and made away with it.

However, his story had two versions: the First Version and a Revised Standard Version. In the First Version, he didn't mention a "pistol". It was in the Revised Standard Version that he made mention of a pistol, just to make the story much more palatable and credible.

Yet, everyone knew the truth. Both Patricia and Fidelis knew he wasn't carrying any passengers and that no one had harassed him with a gun. What he told them was comparable to the type of story anyone who broke a clay pot would always tell; but for the sake of peace and tranquility, they decided to let the sleeping dog lie.

Just as he had finished telling his story, Chiamaka and Nwanyibunwa came back from the bore-hole where they went to fetch water; and when they heard their mother's voice in the room, they quickly emptied their water in the water drum and went in to see whom she was talking with.

'Nne, are you back?' Fidelis asked them as they pushed the entry door open and came in.

'Yes,' they replied and added: 'Dee, good evening, sir!'

'Evening, Nnoo-nu' Fidelis said. "Thank you, sir!' they said. All this while, they didn't know that the person sitting near the refrigerator was their father. Syl himself didn't even raise his face up to see his children whom he had not seen for three whole months. Perhaps he was ashamed of himself. When eventually their mother told them it was their father, they rushed at him, gripped him and nearly pushed him out of his seat.

'Daddy, how're you?' Nwanyibunwa asked him. 'Nne, I'm fine,' he responded quietly.

'And you?' 'I'm fine,' the little girl replied. 'I hope you girls do go to school?' 'Yes, daddy,' the two girls answered in chorus. Almost immediately, Chiamaka asked: 'But daddy, where have you been since?'

'Nne, let's talk about that later,' he parried the question.
'Okay, dad,' the girl accepted and shut her mouth. Fidelis stayed with them till 9pm before he bade them goodnight and went back to his house. On the following day, Patricia left for the market very early. Later, Chiamaka and Nwanyibunwa left for school. Syl was all alone in the house, and there was nothing lef for him to eat. The little food left over the previous nigh was eaten for breakfast by the two girls before the went to school. Patricia was not used to eating at home in the moming. She usually ate her brunch in the market about mid-day.

Syl kept yawning in hunger and, at times, would go to the food cupboard to search for food; but he would see none. Then, he would drink some water.

For three good days, no one asked him whether he would eat or not. He then began to look for a way to fend for himself. He had to go back to the park where he used to work, this time no longer as a driver, but now as a loader. When his colleagues saw him, they welcomed him very warmly asking him where he had been for the past three months. As usual, he told them his cock-and bull stories, though he didn't tell them his car was snatched away from him. If he did, they would laugh at him. Of course, they all knew he sold the car, especially as the fellow that bought it was from the same park.

He simply told them he was sick even to the verge of death. They were all sorry for him, thanking God for his recovery. 'When you were struck with such serious ailment, why didn't you send a message across to us?'

one of his colleagues asked him. Syl laughed and then said, 'Could one stand up, let alone think of sending a message across to you people?' 'I didn't say you should have come yourself, What I mean is that you could have sent either your wife or one of your children to come and let us know At least, one or two persons might have come to see you and know how you were doing,' the fellow said. 'Is my wife, whom you're talking about, not the one that was running up and down looking for a means to treat me? As for my children, they're all still too small to have been sent here from where I'm living,' Syl said in defence. However, some of his colleagues knew that what he was telling them was a mere load of hocus pocus, They knew he didn't take ill, although he looked every inch like someone who had just recovered from a very Serious illness. Did Ala-Owere later not tell them about is encounter with Syl's wife: how the woman came to me park to report that she had not seen her husband for vo days?

Soon, a Mazda car took its turn for loading. Syl loaded it and the driver gave him twenty naira. When another vehicle (Jetta) entered, he also succeeded in loading it. In short, almost every vehicle that loaded in that park that day was handled by Syl, not because he was the smartest, but because of the story he had told, and for the adjunct reason that he looked very hungry. These together made his colleagues decide to concede so much loading responsibility and benefits to him that day.

They wanted to use the day to welcome him back to the park; and by the end of the day, he had made close to eight hundred naira. This time, he didn't drink kinkana (the local gin). He merely ate "mama put" worth of just fifty naira only. After eating the jollof rice, without meat, he didn't even buy sachet water; instead, he requested for a cup of tap water.

He deliberately didn't eat the food in time; but waited till about 4pm so that, if on getting home, his wife didn't give him food in the night, the one he had eaten in the park would sustain him till the next day.

After paying his transport fare back home, he was left with five hundred naira. When his wife came back in the night, he gave her four hundred and fifty naira and kept the remaining fifty naira for his transport fare to work the next day. That night, Patricia managed to give him some food.

On the following day, he went back to the park, but could not make more than one hundred naira which he spent there on the spot: using seventy naira to buy corn and pear and spending the rest on kinkana. He would have trekked back home, but for one of his fellow drivers, Diokpa, who offered him a free ride in his taxi cab.

Every Thursday was sanitation in the market
where Patricia did her business and she
would always use the first half of the day to
do some domestic chores. Therefore, after
Chiamaka and Nwanyibunwa had left For
school, she packed all the dirty clothes in
the house excluding Syl's) outside and
washed them. First, she washed her own
clothes. Next, she washed her aughters'.

After washing the clothes, she washed the
kitchen ensils, including the ones they had
not used since they packed into the house.
She also cleaned the food cupboard and the
refrigerator as well as all the electronic
gadgets in the room. Then, she swept the
room thoroughly, shifting all the chairs, the
center table and the TV stand. Thereafter,
she took her bath in readiness to go to the
market.

On one such a day, after she had completed
all the above, she was ready to leave, but
Syl had not taken his bath. He was still

preparing to do so. Patricia went into the room and ordered him out of the room so that she could lock up the house. He didn't have any choice but to remove the towel he had already tied around his waist in preparation for a bath, put on his clothes, and leave the room. After all, he was not the one paying the rent.

When he had gone out, Patricia locked the house tied the key to her wrapper (as she would always do) and went to the market. Thus, when Syl got home that evening, he couldn't go into the house. He had to sit outside on a log of wood until his family came back from the market.

'Daddy, good evening!' his children managed to greet him when they saw him. Patricia pretended she didn't see him, let alone greet him. She went straight to open the door and enter the house. The two girls followed.

A few minutes after they had gone in, Syl followed

suit. Chiamaka and Nwanyibunwa then went out to

fetch water, while Patricia started to get things ready

for cooking. Syl went into the room, removed his

outing clothes, and tied a towel around his waist, just

as in the morning. He came out, took a plastic bucket

and went to the water drum to fetch some water for

his bath. As he opened the drum, Patricia caught sight
of him.
'Who's at that drum?" she asked pretending she didn't know it was he.

'It's me, Syl', he turned to her and answered. 'Who are you? Sylvanus?' she asked.

'Yes,' he said, 'I want to take some water for my bath.'

'Which water?' she asked. 'Is it the water that these two little children suffered to fetch that you want to use to take your bath? Have you asked whether we've taken our own bath? You've seen some Jackies that fetch water for you, that's why you want to take a bath. By the way, what were you doing throughout the day? Couldn't you have fetched water before we came back? Didn't you see a bucket or haven't you seen your fellow men who fetch water before? I won't blame you, because I rented a house and allowed you into it, That's why you've the guts to say you want to bathe. Don't worry; very soon you'll go back to the village. Your property has gone and you'll soon follow. Give me that bucket, jari!' She snatched the bucket away from him. 'Empty vessel,' she called him as she left him and rushed back to continue her cooking.

Syl was speechless and motionless. What would he say when he couldn't play his role as head of the family. However, he recalled when he was "darling Syl", not now that he was called a mere "Sylvanus" by his wife, without the slightest atom of respect. He recalled when he married Patricia newly and did virtually everything for her, even buying her an SUV Jeep. He now realized, with pain and grief, the trouble with women, namely that the moment any of them becomes the bread-winner of the family she invariably begins to disobey and look down on her husband, to the extent of making him an object of ridicule, even before the children and other family members.

After that most embarrassing and humiliating experience, the poor man shrugged his shoulders and went back quietly to the room without taking his bath.

Chapter Seven

He that controls money controls the mind;
for nothing influences the mind like money
does.
Since the water incident, Syl had not eaten
in his home. He had been doing everything

possible to influence his wife to begin to give him food again. At one time, he had collected all the dirty plates in the house and washed them. At another time, he had washed Patricia's dirty clothes, including her underwears. When the clothes dried, he took them in and ironed those that could be ironed. After that, he folded them carefully and kept them on the bed. In spite of all these, Patricia remained resolute in her decision not to give him her food again. In the circumstance, he continued to go to the motor park for loading taxi cabs, from which he got some token pay for his daily bread. The work had become very competitive, so much so that at times, at the end of the day, he hardly got enough to cover his transport as well as his feeding. This time, even university graduates were competing for the job.

'Since the government has refused to offer me a job, let me do the one that is accessible, at least to keep my stomach warm,' a university graduate had once said.

Syl would not want to go to Fidelis' house to complain to him. He didn't want anyone to begin to ask him if he had been providing for his family, knowing fully well his present economic predicament.

When he was in the airport-taxi work, he had a rich customer who was always very kind to him. Whenever he had any financial problem, he would run to the man and he never failed to bail him out. The problem now, however, was how he could go to New Road where Alfred, his erstwhile customer, lived. He couldn't in fact afford the taxi fare to go there. Was he going to trek the over ten-kilometer distance? Perhaps, he would have done so, but for the fact that he hadn't eaten for five days and so had but very little energy. However, as a veteran smart guy, he convinced himself that he could still hustle his way through any tight situation, such as the present one.
So, after Patricia and her daughters had left for the market that Saturday morning, Syl

took his bath, dressed up, locked the entrance door and left for the central motor park. There he boarded a taxi that was going to New Road. As they moved, passengers dropped while new ones entered. There was a young man sitting next to him in the back seat. He wore a pair of washed jeans trousers and a face cap that almost covered his face. After about eight kilometers, the young man suddenly called the attention of the driver.

'Yes?' the driver answered.

'I get wetin I want tell you,' the young man said. "Yes? Wetin be dat?' asked the driver, 'I wan tell you say I go drop for First Transformer,' the young man said.

By then, they had passed the First Transformer he was talking about and were almost at the Second Transformer. You know say you go drop for First transformer, why you no talk am in time?' the driver blamed the young man while clearing from the main road. When he had pulled up, he asked the young man to drop, but the latter refused asking the driver: 'Na here I tell you say, I go drop, abi you no sabi First Transformer again?' 'Wetin you wan make I do? Abi you tell me in time say na there you go drop?' the driver asked him. 'I no tell you in time?,' the young man queried and further asked, 'Abi dis no be your route?' 'How I go know where you wan drop when you no talk as we reach there?' the driver asked.

'Na me go tell you?' the young man asked. You suppose to tell me,' the driver argued, 'Abi no be so?' he turned to the other passengers and asked.

They all affirmed that the onus was on any passenger
to tell the driver (in advance) where and when they wanted to drop.

Okay now, carry me de go wherever you de go as you no sabi your work again. When you don taya, you go come drop me for de correct place,' the young man said and relaxed himself in the car.

Meanwhile, the other four passengers (including Syl) were beginning to feel uncomfortable as their movement was being delayed. They all joined the driver in persuading the young man to drop where the driver had stopped for him instead of arguing over who was at fault. Eventually, it happened that the driver must concede the two hundred naira which the young man was to pay him (as the latter had entered from the park). Otherwise, he would have to reverse to drop him where he said he would drop which was about half a kilometer back. In the ensuing stalemate, the driver chose the first option, that even if he went back and dropped the young man where he was insisting on, the latter might still not pay him. 'Oya, go! Go! Go!' he thus said to him.

Immediately, the young man jacked the door open, went down and slammed the door back. 'Bagar! I think say you sabi something,' he said to the driver.

'Carry your wahala de go. Idiot!' the driver responded to him in turn as he drove off in anger. Little did he know that another unexpected embarrassment was in the offing. 'Dropping dey!' Syl said aloud to the driver as they got to New Road junction. As usual, the driver cleared from the road and pulled up. Syl jacked the door open; and when he alighted, he began to fumble frantically in his pockets. He combed from his shirt's pockets to the trousers'; but in the end, he couldn't find any money.
Oga, pay me now make I de go! Abi you wan play your own guy trick like the other man? the driver asked him.

'Na the five hundred naira wey I carry na him I de find so,' Syl said, still fumbling in his pockets.

'Which kind yeye talk be that one? I beg, pay me my money make I commot,' the driver said, turning off the ignition and alighting from the car. He went up to where Syl was standing and widened up his palm demanding for his money. Before Syl knew what was happening, he had hel fast to his belt. 'Give me my money!' he screamed at him.There was another young man sitting in the front seat who probably sympathized with Syl's plight. He called the driver and asked him how much was Syl's money.

"Two hundred naira,' the driver said still holding Syl by the belt.

'Don't worry, I'll give it to you,' the passenger pledged but the driver refused to let go his grip on Syl's belt.

'Make you give me the money now,' he insisted. When the "Good Samaritan" discovered that the driver was not willing to let go his hold on Syl unless he got the money, he brought out two hundred naira and gave it to the driver.

'God don save you,' the driver said as he released Syl.

'Bro, thank you,' Syl said to the 'Good Samaritan'. 'Not to worry,' the man responded. Syl didn't go his way immediately. He stood with hands crossed watching the driver pull the vehicle back to the tarred road. Meanwhile, he imagined what would have become of him had the "Good Samaritan" not come to his rescue: how the driver would have pounced on him and devoured him like a hungry lion. In all, he thanked God for His grace upon his life that morning.

When the cab had virtually driven off, Syl waved at his rescuer and then crossed over to the other side of the road to join the New Road in question. As he walked, he

staggered forth and back as hunger was
written all over his body.

Alfred was living at No 19 New Road when
Syl visited him last. Syl had every hope that
he was still living there, but that hope was
soon dashed.

There was a bell at the gate of No. 19 New
Road. When Syl got to the gate, he pressed
the bell and soon sommeone emerged from
inside and opened the gate.
'Baby, how are you?' Syl asked the little girl.
'Fine!' she said and added: 'Good morning,
sir!'

'Morning! What of your dad?'

'He's fine.'

'Hope you're Chief Alfred's daughter?'

'No!' the girl said and added: 'My daddy's
name is Gilbert.'

Upon hearing this, Syl became nervous. He imagined how he would trek back home when he was totally listless and could hardly stand on his feet. In the alternative, he would have to repeat the same tricks he had played when he was coming. What if he wasn't as fortunate as he was earlier to find someone who would bail him out? What if, this time the driver happened to be an ill-tempered person who might give him a heavy blow when he had not eaten for the past five days; wouldn't he fall down and faint?

To clear every atom of doubt, he asked the little girl to go and call her father. She went in and soon came out with a man. As soon as Syl saw the man, he began to melt up like a piece of rubber put in the fire. He knew he was finished and would definitely go back home on foot; and now that he was extremely hungry, he wasn't sure he would be able to make it. 'So, what this girl said is true,' he had said in his mind.

'Good day!' Gilbert greeted.

'Good day, sir; and how is everything?" Syl responded.
'It's well,' Gilbert said.

'Please, I'm looking for one man who lives here,"
Syl said. 'What's the person's name?'
Gilbert asked.
'His name is Alfred,' Syl answered. 'I don't know any such name.' Gilbert said. 'But he used to live here', Syl insisted. 'Or is this place not No 19?' he asked

'Of course, it is,' Gilbert said, and added: 'Perhaps he's the person that packed out before I moved in.' 'But when I used to visit him, he told me he was the owner of this place,' said Syl.

'I wouldn't know,' Gilbert said. 'All I know is that I didn't meet anyone here when I came in and the person that let the place to me never told me who was formerly occupying it.'

'Is he tall and dark: I mean your landlord?' Syl asked.

'No, he's short and very fair,' Gilbert said, then went on to ask: 'But Oga, does the fellow you're looking for not have a phone? Can't you call him on phone?' 'I don't have his number,' Syl said after a sigh.
Truly, he used to have Alfred's phone number, but the phone in which he saved the number was later stolen.

'If you had his number, you would've just called him to know his whereabouts,' Gilbert said.

'No, I don't have his number,' Syl said shaking his head.

'Alright then!' Gilbert said and withdrew back to his house. Meanwhile, his daughter followed him shutting the gate behind her. Syl stood with hands akimbo, his eyes to the heavens. For the second time in his lifetime, he saw the sun set in broad daylight. The first time he had a comparable experience was when he was sacked from work in the oil company.

After tarrying for a while, he left the No. 19 gate and walked back very slowly towards the road junction. By the time he got to the junction, he was virtually completely exhausted.
At the junction was a concrete electric pole that was lying parallel to the expressway. He sat down on the pole. If any vehicle passed, he turned and looked at it, trying to see whether he could identify either the vehicle or its driver. Till 4:30pm, he was still at the junction; and by then, he had given up every hope of going back home. So, he kept turning his eyes in curiosity for any vacant

shop where he could pass the night. Just then, a Passat wagon car, passed. Soon, the vehicle pulled up and came back with the reverse gear.

'Oga Winter, wetin you de find here?' the cab driver asked loudly while peeping out via the passenger's door.

'Who de call me so?" Syl asked, while he struggled to know who it was.

When the driver realized that he didn't know who was calling him, he turned off the ignition, came down and went up to him.

'Oh! Alfonso,' Syl exclaimed as he saw the driver clearly 'na you?'

Oga Winter! Alfonso called him and asked again:
'Wetin you de do here?' 'My broda, na so I see am today,' he replied with a faint smile. As you no carry passengers where you de

come from?' he asked. 'Oga Winter,. I just
dey look for passengers. Wetin you say you
de do here?' he asked for the third time.

'My broda, I come see my friend for New
Road here. As I de come, I loss the money
wey I wan use enter taxi. Na free lift I been
de look for since."

'How manage you loss the money?' Alfonso
asked. 'My broda, the thing taya me,' Syl
said. 'I put am for pocket. I no know say the
pocket get hole. As I come down from taxi
wey I enter for Mile Three park, I put hand
for my pocket to bring out money to pay the
driver; I no see the money again.'

'How much be that?' Alfonso asked him.
'Na two thousand naira,' he said.

Alfonso laughed in his mind. He knew Syl's
hand had not touched five hundred naira for
the past one month, not to talk of having two
thousand naira in his pocket. Nevertheless,

he didn't argue with him. He simply asked him to enter the car. As Syl stood up to enter the car, all his whole body was shaking.

Oga Winter, you dey well at all?' Alfonso asked him.

'My broda, I' dey well,' he sighed and said.

'Wetin make your body de shake like this now? You don chop?'

The money wey I for take chop, no be the one wey loss?

'You no chop before you commot for morning?' 'My broda, I chop, but it don tee now, since early momo."

Alfonso guessed that he didn't eat before he left home in the morning. Had he eaten, he wouldn't have been looking so weak, he imagined. Therefore, as soon as he saw a restaurant, Alfonso cleared from the main road, pulled up and turned off the car ignition. Both of them alighted from the car and went into the restaurant.

"Una get food?' Alfonso asked a young girl they met in the restaurant.

'Yes,' replied the girl.

'Wetin una get? he asked

"We get fufu, we get garri, we get rice,' she replied 'Oga Winter, wetin you wan chop? he asked Syl.

'Una get draw soup?' Syl asked the young girl. 'Na egusi and vegetable we get,' the girl replied. 'Mix am for me,' said Syl.

'Garri abi fufu?' the girl asked him 'Fufu,' he requested
After taking the food order, the girl came back in a short while carrying a plastic bowl

with some water in it and sachet water in a small plastic plate. She kept them on a white circular table and went immediately for the food. Before she came back, Syl had already washed his hands. Thus, as soon as the food was placed on the table, he pounced on it and in less than five minutes, he levelled the mountain of fufu (pounded cassava) that had been loaded for him.

'Make them bring extra?' Alfonso asked him.

Though he didn't say yes, Alfonso knew he needed more food; and so he asked the girl to serve him an extra half plate. She went over the counter and soon came back carrying two ceramic plates containing soup and fufu, respectively. She turned the soup into the soup plate already on the table and the fufu, into the other plate. Syl rushed through the extra food and finished it in the blink of an eye. As he washed his hands, Alfonso paid the bill. He gave the young girl five hundred naira note and collected his one hundred and fifty naira change.

'My brother, you don save me today,' Syl said to Alfonso after drinking the sachet water. Wetin I do for you sef?' Alfonso asked and added: 'Na wetin man fit do for him friend' be dat.'

Thank you plenty, plenty, Syl said.

'Don't mention,' Alfonso said.

"Anything remain? Make we de go. Alfonso said standing up to go.

'Nothing!' said Syl while struggling to stand up; and just then, he coughed.

'You get cough?' Alfonso asked

'No-o!' he replied. I just de see this one now.'

As he was still talking, he coughed again; and then vomitted blood. Alfonso gripped him.

'Oga Winter, wetin be this?' he asked him. 'I no know-o!' Syl managed to reply in a weak and faint voice. Then, he vomitted blood again and slumped. Alfonso shouted, and people gathered immediately and helped him put Syl in the car. He rushed to the steering, and zoomed off to a hospital.

Unfortunately, the near-by private hospital could not be of help as the Medical Director was not available and the nurse on duty was afraid to initiate any treatment without instructions and prescriptions from her boss. So, she directed them to a government hospital which was about five kilometers away.

Alfonso took off immediately at a blistering speed; but before he got to the said General Hospital, Syl was already gasping for breath. He was however admitted and the doctors battled to see if they could do anything to revive him; but alas, it was too late.

When Patricia heard the news, she abandoned all she was doing in the market and rushed to the hospital.

'Who killed my husband?" she raved as she got to the room where Syl's corpse was kept.

'Madam, nobody killed him,' the Chief Medical Director of the hospital told her and then added:
'However, the diagnosis we've carried out reveals that he didn't eat for a very long time; and when eventually he did, he didn't drink some water first before going for a heavy meal."

As soon as she heard this, she covered her mouth with her hands and resorted to weeping. She knew she was pretty guilty of the reported starvation; so she withheld her strong suspicion of some diabolic foul play by Alfonso and the other new-found friends and associates of her deceased husband.

She wept and wept and wept; but it was not clear, whether her continuous weeping was springing from deep sorrow or heartfelt remorse; or she was merely shedding crocodile tears.

The corps of Syl was in the mortuary for more than three months, before scanty resources could eventually be put together for its burial: a shabby burial, characterized by unimpressive funeral rites.

www.ingramcontent.com/pod-product-compliance
Lightning Source LLC
Chambersburg PA
CBHW071322140726
47996CB00005B/1770